This was just

She was known t...
ready to take cha... ...able to
anything. No one knew—was entitled to
know—how she felt underneath.

For a moment that lasted an eternity they
looked at each other. Then he bent his head to
kiss her.

'Perhaps I should say I am sorry?' he
whispered.

'Whatever happened, it was as much my fault
as yours. I wanted you. But…we had to stop.
Kissing is one thing, and it was lovely, but I
can't give you more than that.'

Gill Sanderson is a psychologist who finds time to write only by staying up late at night. Weekends are filled by her hobbies of gardening, running and mountain walking. Her ideas come from her work, from one son who is an oncologist, one son who is a nurse and her daughter who is a trainee midwife. She first wrote articles for learned journals and chapters for a textbook. Then she was encouraged to change to fiction by her husband, who is an established writer of war stories.

Recent titles by the same author:

A FAMILY TO SHARE

A FAMILY AGAIN

BY
GILL SANDERSON

MILLS & BOON®

To the BA honours midwifery class of 1995, John Moores University.

First published in Great Britain 1998
Harlequin Mills & Boon Limited,
Eton House, 18-24 Paradise Road, Richmond, Surrey TW9 1SR

© Gill Sanderson 1998

ISBN 0 263 81242 1

Set in Times Roman 11 on 12 pt.
03-9810-48009-D

Printed and bound in Norway
by AiT Trondheim AS, Trondheim

CHAPTER ONE

THEY met by coincidence. Afterwards, when she looked back on that first magic encounter, Emily thought she'd known at once that this was the man for her. Perhaps she had. But it was a long time before she'd fully realised it.

The hut roof was filled with acrid smoke from a tiny fire, and two hurricane lamps shed a scarely adequate light. Emily's patient, Nupala, had been in labour all night, and now the contractions were only five minutes apart. Nupala leaned patiently against the hut wall, only the odd hiss of breath and the sweat on her forehead indicating how she felt. Women did not cry in labour.

Two older women squatted to one side of the hut, fanning away the flies. They were Nupala's mother and mother-in-law, and they had spent much of the night rubbing Nupala's abdomen, so much so, in fact, that Emily had asked them to stop. The skin was almost abrading.

Emily's trainee midwife, Eunice Latifa, was kneeling on the packed-mud floor, leaning over to listen to the baby's heartbeat with a Pinard stethoscope. Good variability with slight accelerations, returning quickly to the baseline. The baby wasn't in distress.

There were no partograms here to record the baby's progress. Emily looked at Eunice's notebook, and nodded approvingly. One of the hardest lessons to get over was the necessity for writing down the results of every investigation or observation immediately.

All the trainees at the mission felt that they were to be nurses or midwives, not clerks. They didn't like writing—especially when they were recording that everything was normal. Emily smiled wryly. She could think of quite a few colleagues in far-off England who thought the same way.

But Eunice had diligently recorded temperature, blood pressure, pulse and foetal heart rate. She had checked that the bladder had been emptied regularly. She had carefully tested Nupala's urine, which showed no signs of ketones or protein.

Eunice was anxious, not about the birth but about the fact that her tutor was observing her. Somehow her anxiety was communicating itself to the patient. Nupala was more restless than was necessary.

'I'm just going outside a minute, Eunice,' Emily said. 'You're doing fine—you don't need me.'

Great dark eyes flashed at her anxiously. 'Call if you want me,' Emily added gently, 'but I see no reason why you shouldn't carry on by yourself.'

Eunice took this as it had been intended, as a signal of confidence in her work. 'Yes, Mis' Grey,' she said. 'But I think this baby doing fine.'

Outside it was nearly dawn, and there was a lightening in the eastern sky. Emily looked at the conical huts, huddled in a circle, and the thorn trees that surrounded the settlement. There were sounds—the thump of cattle feet in their enclosure, the cackle of hens, roosting in the trees. And everywhere there was the smell of Africa—part wood-smoke, part cattle dung, part vegetation. It was instantly recognisable, instantly evocative. It had been part of her life for two years now.

She breathed deeply and for a moment stretched her arms over her head, enjoying the coolness. She'd been up all night and she was tired. But, then, she was always tired.

It shot through her unexpectedly, as sharp as a scalpel. And for her it was the rarest of things. She was homesick. Instead of the brightness of Africa, she wanted the muted colours of home. She wanted a duller sun, a more gentle rain. She wanted the company of her own kind. She wanted to see her father and her two sisters. She wanted to practise medicine again in a full-sized hospital where there were doctors and consultants—people she could refer to who would take responsibility. She didn't like taking so many decisions. She grimaced. She had to take decisions. Often there was no one else to do it.

Behind her she heard excited whispers and a gasp from Nupala. The birth would be soon. She slipped back inside the hut and deliberately stood well back. Eunice must do this by herself.

The two old ladies moved forward and Eunice smartly waved them back. She would handle this birth. She spoke to the panting mother in the local tongue. Emily had learned enough to make herself understood, but could not talk with any speed.

There was a quick rapped command. Emily hid a grin. 'Push,' must sound the same in any language. Approvingly she noticed how Eunice had positioned herself to receive the baby.

There was a sound, half sob, half moan, from

Nupala. Her legs spread wide. After fifteen minutes
the head was showing. Deftly Eunice placed her hand
on the head to guide it. The mother was told to pant
as Eunice gently eased the head out, sweeping the
perineum. She checked the cord wasn't round the
baby's neck. The rest of the procedure was followed
correctly, and soon the little body was born. It was a
boy. That would please the family as boys were more
use than girls. Eunice wrapped him in the cloth she'd
put handy, then placed him on his mother's breast.

Next she clipped and then cut the umbilical cord.
Emily heard the hiss of dismay from the two ladies.
The local custom was to leave the baby attached until
the placenta was delivered.

Methodically Eunice went about her tasks, as she
had been taught. The placenta was delivered and
checked. One of the ladies took possession of it at
once. Emily knew what would happen to it. It would
be buried secretly, as would be all the blood that
Nupala had lost. A witch-doctor could do great harm
with a placenta.

Emily loved being a midwife—in England or in
Africa. Even after so many births, the moment a new,
healthy baby was placed on the mother's breast was
still magic for her. It was a joy she'd never had. For
a second she was tormented by the thought of what
might have been. What was it like to give birth to a
new life? But she thrust the thought aside. She was
tired, that was all.

Now was the time for the family to come to con-
gratulate Nupala. Emily took Eunice to one side and
gave her report. Eunice had done well and Emily con-
gratulated her. The only fault she had found was that

Eunice hadn't made sufficient use of the two old ladies. 'They probably could have managed quite well without us,' Emily said. 'After all, they've been doing it for years.'

'Not the hospital way,' Eunice said proudly.

Nupala was now in the care of her family. She would be wrapped in a blanket so that only her eyes could be seen. She would stay in her hut for the next two months, the baby never leaving her side. Her mother would feed her maize-meal and millet porridge, trying to ensure that Nupala put on weight. Emily guessed that there were worse ways of starting life with a baby. She went to find her own breakfast.

After breakfast there was a clinic. She'd trained as a nurse before she became a midwife, and although she was technically with the mission as a midwife no one paid much attention to demarcation.

A hut had been put at her disposal, with a long line of patiently queueing clients outside. She sighed. Some of the decisions she was about to make should really be taken by a doctor. But the nearest doctor was in the mission hospital over a hundred miles away. And he was busy. If necessary, her patients could make their way to the mission, but they'd prefer to stay where they were. And if they thought they were cured—if the symptoms ceased—then so would taking the medicine cease. She sighed again. All you could do was your best.

Her boxes of medicine had been put ready, as well as a bucket of water, should she need it. There was sulphur ointment for scabies, vitamin tablets and syrup for the undernourished children and pregnant women and penicillin injections for those with venereal disease or acute infections. She also kept a good supply of dressings for children with burns. At night the younger children tended to roll into the fire in the centre of the hut.

She had already injected as many as she could find with the BCG vaccine against tuberculosis. Tuberculosis was one of the biggest killers in the crowded, often unsanitary conditions of the villages.

The morning clinic was quickly over. Emily knew she had to be ruthless with her time. Everyone had thoroughly enjoyed themselves—a visit to the doctor was fun. After prescriptions had been issued there was always a keen comparison of who had been given what medicine. There was even a selection of placebos for those who had nothing wrong with them but wanted to have medicine anyway. She could have stayed there indefinitely, but that was always the problem. There was never enough time.

There were two more babies due later on in the week, and one a month or so later. With Eunice, Emily examined the first two mums. Everything seemed to be fine. The third one she wasn't so sure about. It was primigravida—the lie seemed to be oblique and the foetal head remained unengaged.

'Tell Serwalo that she must come into hospital in two weeks' time,' Emily said to Eunice. 'We wish her to have her baby there.'

Eunice spoke quickly to the recumbent woman, who looked anxious. 'She says she will be happy to come to hospital. Her husband will bring her in the oxcart,' Eunice translated. 'This is her first baby and she and her husband have been trying for too long.

She says if she does not give him a baby he will leave her because she is barren.'

Emily's first reaction was anger, though not surprise. If a woman didn't have babies it was always considered her fault, never the husband's. Then she reminded herself that this was Africa, not England, and things were different here. Her job was to help, not to judge.

'Tell her we'll do all we can,' she said. 'And she must keep taking the supplements we've left her.' She would have liked to take Serwalo back to the hospital with her but pregnant women were still expected to work in the village. She would refuse to come.

It was time to leave. She looked at Eunice's supplies, spoke to the headman of the village and loaded her few personal possessions into the Land Rover. There was so much more she could do if she stayed here. But this was only one village, and there were many others.

'I have confidence in you, Eunice,' she said. 'You will do well with these two births. In a fortnight a Land Rover will come to fetch you and I will see the two fine babies you have helped into the world. You must have confidence in yourself.'

'I will do as you tell me Mis' Grey,' said Eunice stoutly. 'These babies will be born well.'

'I'm sure they will. You're going to be a good midwife, Eunice.' Emily hauled herself into the vehicle. One last wave and she bumped slowly away. Naked little boys chased after her, cheering, and for the first few yards she drove slowly. Then they fell behind and she increased speed.

The Land Rover was old and battered, the name of

the mission on the side almost hidden by caked dust. When she'd first arrived at the hospital Sister O'Reilly had given her a crash course in elementary mechanics. If you broke down in the bush you had to mend things yourself. Emily had got quite attached to her old machine. She now knew nearly as much about what happened under its bonnet as she did about delivering babies. And the mission was having a new one delivered next week.

The track she followed was deeply rutted, and for the first fifteen miles the vehicle bounced and swayed. She was jerked and thrown against her seat—driving in these conditions could be as tiring as cross-country running. Then she turned onto a road that was more regularly used so it was smoother. Still not the M1, she thought.

Emily was hot and she was exhausted, with the bone-weary exhaustion that came with months of too much work. Her arms were thin but sinewy, and her legs were the same. She looked like a greyhound. Greyhound? Her name was Grey—there was a joke there. She found herself laughing, then thought she was laughing too much. It wasn't that funny. She was being hysterical. Exerting her usual iron self-control, she stopped laughing and concentrated on the route ahead.

She dropped out of the bush and was now following the road across a hot dry plain. Behind her a plume of yellow dust hung in the air. There was some coolness in the wind she was creating, but she could feel the dust, collecting in her nostrils and the corners of her eyes and rubbing at her skin. No matter. This was normal. She'd shower when she got back to the mission.

Ahead of her was a great ridge of mountains. After an hour her route swung up and over it, to drop down into the valley on the far side. As she climbed the temperature dropped. It wasn't exactly cool but it was certainly cooler. There was less vegetation now, more red-black rocks. This was an old volcanic range.

She thought of holidays in her youth, of travelling by car through the Welsh mountains to get to the seaside resorts of Caernarvon or Conway. She'd bathed there with her father and sisters. It was that memory that made her think of the pool.

She was making good time. At the top of the pass that crossed the mountains she pulled in to look at the vast plain below her. On each side of the road dark crags loomed, but to her left there was the roughest of paths, leading higher. She'd driven up it before. On impulse she wrenched at the wheel and headed for the track. She'd do something mad for an hour!

For twenty minutes she threaded her way upwards. Then she turned by a great boulder—and in front of her was a tiny blue lake.

Sister O'Reilly had brought her here once with a group of children. They'd never seen so much water. They'd run and paddled, and then shrieked at the coldness of it.

Usually it wasn't safe to swim in any open stretch of African water. The danger from Bilharziasis, a disease carried by a water-borne parasite, was far too great. But it was known that this cold volcanic pool was free of it.

She parked in the shade of the boulder. There was

no one around—there never was. For a minute she just sat, enjoying the peace—the unusual pleasure of having no one near her, no one waiting for her.

From her bag in the back she took a towel and stretched it over the steering-wheel. Then she slipped out of sandals, shorts and shirt. One last look round, and she walked down the coarse sand beach and into the water.

It was cold—a most unusual sensation. She began to swim, a half-remembered splashy crawl. This was glorious!

For four hours Dr Stephen James had driven over the dusty plain from the town of Golanda. He was enjoying himself. This was a new experience—he'd never driven so far and seen so few people—but now he was getting a little tired. He hadn't stopped on the plain, one reason being that it all looked the same. Why pick one place to stop and not another?

The new Land Rover was easy to drive, but crammed full of medical supplies. He wondered what the mission would be like, so far from civilisation. That was why he was going—to see medicine practised out in the bush. He'd never felt so alone. And he rather liked it.

Ahead was a dark mountain range, and the road seemed to lead right to it. He stopped to consult his map, though it wasn't really necessary as there was only one road. But he liked to know where he was. He calculated that he had a couple more hours' driving time. He'd driven himself and his vehicle hard. But, then, he always did. Work hard, play hard.

He climbed out of the Land Rover, stretched and

took great breaths of the strange-scented air. On the dashboard was a letter, and he reached through the window to read it again. It was from Lyn Taylor, whom he'd known for years. He liked people who were determined, hard-working, even ambitious. And Lyn was all of those. In some ways she was like himself.

He'd first met her eight years ago when she'd been a staff nurse in the London hospital where he'd got his first registrar's job. She'd told him she wanted to be a doctor, and was studying A levels at night school. He'd helped her with her studies, even though he'd been busy, studying himself, and he'd seen that she got a good recommendation to medical school. She'd been accepted by a northern university, she'd written to him frequently and they'd met on occasion. Both had been working furiously.

Now she was qualified, and had written to say she'd got a house position on his firm. He had just been appointed Specialist Registrar in Gynaecology at Blazes Hospital. It would be good to work together.

He might need friends in this new job. He would have to prove himself—too many people would say that he was trading on his father's reputation. He didn't think he was. Frowning, he threw down the letter and climbed in to restart the engine.

After another half-hour he came to the foot of the dark mountain range he'd seen ahead. The gradient wasn't too bad, though there were plenty of rocks on the road, and he bumped upwards cautiously. The yellow dust disappeared—here there was only black volcanic grit.

It grew cooler, too. He felt grateful as he wasn't

used to this constant heat. He eased forward, trying to pull his shirt away from his sticky skin.

Finally he reached the top of the pass, and stopped to stare at the long vista ahead. He climbed out of the vehicle, and stretched his arms and legs again. So much wild country—and no sign of life! He shook his head in astonishment.

His feet crunched on the volcanic ash, so different from the powdery dust of the plain. He looked downwards, and to his surprise saw tyre tracks in the dust. They looked recent. And they led off the main track and curved upwards.

Puzzled, he turned to his map. Yes, there was something marked, though scarcely a main road, and it led to a tiny marked lake. He wondered who could be ahead. Traffic up here wasn't exactly heavy. He had passed several ox carts and just two ancient lorries, loaded to an incredible degree with animals and people. But that was some time ago, nearer the main town. Who could have driven up this track? He wanted to find out.

Carefully he drove upwards. He rounded a giant boulder, and there in its shade was another Land Rover, with a similar logo to the one on his own vehicle. Ahead was an impossibly blue pool, reflecting the dark peaks beyond. And there was someone swimming in the pool.

The water seemed to be near freezing—swimming in it was a totally new experience for Emily in Africa. She hadn't swum for two years, and after the initial yelp of horror at the temperature she revelled in it. In another life she'd been quite a good swimmer, school champion, in fact. She felt some of her cares and worries melt away as her body adapted to the coolness and the exercise. She felt good.

She was only in the water for twenty minutes. It would have been foolish to stay in too long. Alone as she was, she couldn't risk getting cramp. Thinking that she must come here again—if ever she had the time—she paddled out onto the black shingle beach and back towards her vehicle. It was out of sight behind the great boulder.

She rounded the boulder, and there was her Land Rover. But there was another one next to it, a newer one. Standing by it was a man, wearing shorts and stripped to the waist.

She was shocked, and as a reflex defensive measure her hands and arms crossed, but not over her bra and briefs. Fortunately, her underwear was of strong cotton and the water hadn't made it transparent. Her arms crossed instead over her abdomen.

She looked at the man and met his level gaze. A flurry of unspoken messages passed between them.

'I didn't mean to disturb you,' he said. 'I'm Dr Stephen James. I'm on my way to the mission. Like you, in fact.'

'I know who you are. We've been expecting you.' She forced herself to move her arms, to let them rest by her side. She felt foolish in this self-protective stance. Her body was white, unlike her sun-browned arms, legs and face. And her abdomen was slashed with ugly red scars.

CHAPTER TWO

STEPHEN'S eyes flickered at Emily's deliberate gesture, and she reddened slightly. She knew he had noticed her scars and guessed he'd recognised them for what they were—part accident, part emergency surgery.

But he retained the usual impassive doctor's face. She was glad. She didn't, of course, expect him to show surprise but neither did she want sympathy.

What did he think of her? she wondered. Once, she knew without arrogance, she'd been a striking girl. Men would turn to look after her in the street. Now, quite simply, she was too thin. Her underwear was sensible but plain. Her best feature, her rich auburn hair, now hung down in wet rat's tails. She hadn't expected to want to impress anyone. She hadn't expected to meet anyone.

Obviously he'd decided not to mention her unconventional swimming gear. This pleased her, though she wouldn't have minded if he had. He offered her the towel she'd placed ready. 'I didn't mean to disturb you,' he said. 'I'll go for a swim myself while you change.'

Then he looked at her—with some anxiety, she thought. 'You will still be here when I come back? You don't have to run away.'

'No, I'll still be here. I'm Emily Grey, by the way. I'm a midwife.'

18

He took her outstretched hand. She felt wet, he felt warm. But some kind of message passed as they stood there with their hands clasped. There was a moment's silence.

He's got a good face, she thought. There was nothing at first unusual about it, apart from the generous mouth and white teeth. But it was a face that inspired confidence. You could trust a man with a face like his. It was reassuring in its ordinariness. And as she gazed longer she decided it wasn't an ordinary face at all.

With a slight shock she realised what she had just thought. She had thought that here was a man you could trust. Emily didn't trust men.

His body was well muscled, with the rangy lines of a runner. Like her, there wasn't an ounce of fat on him. As she noticed this she wondered if he, too, was driven, like her—had his own particular demons, as she had hers. For his sake she hoped not.

With apparent reluctance he let go of her hand. 'I won't be long,' he said, then turned and ran down the beach. He ran easily, as if he was used to it, but with the slightest of limps. She liked seeing him move.

She watched as he splashed into the water, then dived forward to start a fast crawl. He swam as well as he ran—an athlete.

She took her bag into the shade of the boulder, out of sight of the lake, and rooted through it for her deodorant and fresh underwear. She had to put on her old T-shirt and shorts as she had nothing else clean. After she'd dragged a comb through her wet hair she managed to make it look slightly more presentable.

Then she sat in the shade to wait for him. After the

long drive and the swim she had expected to feel tired,
feel like sleeping. Instead, she was mildly excited. She
wanted to talk some more to Dr James'—Stephen, he'd
called himself.

Irritated by her excitement, she told herself that it
was just the novelty. She hadn't seen a man she'd
been attracted to for over two years. In fact, she'd
seen hardly any presentable men at all. And that was
how she liked it. She needed to keep her misery to
herself. She neither needed nor wanted the company
of presentable men.

But…she liked this man. She didn't mind him seeing her in her underwear—didn't feel threatened.
There was kindness in him. She shook herself, an-
noyed. She'd only met him for two minutes. How
could she know what he was like?

He came back up the beach. She wondered if he'd
cut short his swim to come back to talk to her, and
yet again told herself not to be so foolish.

As he came closer she saw that his limp was more
pronounced, and when she could pick out details she
saw that there were angry blue marks on his right
thigh and on his ribs.

'What happened to you?' she asked as he came up
to her and reached for his own towel. 'You're quite
badly bruised.'

He grinned. 'Three games of rugby in four days,
and another two games next week. I'm a forward,
meant to run fast to keep out of trouble. But it doesn't
always work. And the players here are hard!'

She was disappointed. 'I thought you were here as
a doctor, not a rugby player.'

'You can be both, you know. I'm the captain of a

side of medical men—we call ourselves the Hypodermic Irregulars. We're on a month's tour of the area.'

Her mouth turned down. Glancing at him, she knew he'd noticed her disapproval. 'This bit of Africa needs doctors more than it needs rugby players.' It came out harsher than she'd intended.

He'd finished drying himself, rubbing the moisture from his broad shoulders and muscular chest. He turned and squatted lithely beside her, an easy, graceful movement. Apparently he didn't hold her disapproval against her.

'In the last eighteen months, Emily, I've had exactly nine days' holiday. I needed a break. Work too hard and you get stale—inefficient, even.'

He was right, of course. She smiled. 'I know. I'm afraid I get a bit judgemental at times. I'm sorry.' She moved sideways. 'Come and sit on my blanket.'

He was still almost naked, the tight blue shorts doing little to conceal his masculinity. She saw a gleaming drop of water fall from his hair and run down his shoulder and arm. She noted the fine, almost invisible hair on his chest, which narrowed to a thin line, disappearing into his waistband.

It hit her like a blow, so suddenly and unexpectedly that for a moment she could hardly draw breath. He was attractive. He was attractive to *her*! Disbelief flooded through her. She hadn't felt anything like this for over two years. She tried to tell herself that it was simply fatigue, that and the fact that she hadn't met anyone like this for so long.

His eyes were on her, and she strove for something

to say. But he spoke first. 'How long since you ate?' he asked.

The question surprised her. Had she really been assisting at a birth early this morning? She'd eaten only a light breakfast since then.

'I'll get something back at the mission,' she said.

'You need energy now.' He swung to his feet, and went and rummaged in the back of his Land Rover. 'Here, we'll share these.' He returned with a foil-wrapped packet of sandwiches and a bottle of orange juice.

'I can't eat your lunch,' she said, pushing the offered sandwiches away. 'You need it yourself.'

He shook his head. 'I'm sure you'll feed me when we get to the mission. And the hospital in Golanda seems to have an exaggerated idea of what a rugby player can eat. I'll never finish these.'

So she took a sandwich, tried it and discovered she was really hungry. They sat side by side, eating in happy companionship. It was quite cool in the shade, and a mountain breeze caressed them gently.

'I feel like I'm playing truant,' she said, 'and just for once I'm enjoying the feeling.'

'So you don't get to play truant very often?'

She shook her head. 'No. There's always so much to do and so little time. We all have to force ourselves to take a break occasionally but we're always aware that, well, there's someone needing help and you're not giving it to them.'

'That's true of all medicine. How did you know I was Stephen James?'

She smiled. 'We've talked of little else over the past few days. A senior British doctor, a gynaecologist, in fact, visiting our mission to see how we work. We've been arranging visits from all our troublesome cases in all the local villages.'

He looked alarmed but resigned. 'I was invited to deliver the new Land Rover,' he said, 'but I think the idea was that I should just have a gentle look around. A bit of rest and recuperation, in fact. I'm not even sure I'm licensed or insured to practise in this country.'

Emily smiled again, but to herself this time. 'Just wait till you meet Sister O'Reilly,' she said. 'She'll let you do whatever you want. But somehow it'll be what she wants, too.'

'Ah. I've met ward sisters like that before. Frighten the life out of poor junior doctors.'

She giggled. He didn't look as if he'd be easily frightened.

'So where do you fit into the mission hospital?' he asked. 'I know you're a midwife, but who else is there?'

It was only a tiny mission hospital—a health centre, really, rather than a hospital. 'Well, there's Sam Mugumo. He's a doctor and he's in charge. Sister O'Reilly is in charge of the nursing care, and she does some teaching. We have a dozen trainee nurses. I'm the midwife, but I'm supposed to teach midwifery as much as act as one myself. There's a lot of ancillary staff, and that's it.'

He mused over this. 'I would have thought that, for such a tiny staff, practising medicine would have been enough. But you have to teach as well.'

'We like it,' she said swiftly. 'It's satisfying to pass on skills. Sister says that when she gets things working her way she'll go back to Ireland and take Sam with her. But I doubt she'll ever go back.'

There was always so much to do. It was the hardest thing in the world to refuse to help when you knew you could make a difference.

'Sister told me when I came that I had to prioritise,' she went on. 'It's a nasty word for a nasty thing. But we do it. We have to. We might not help an old man as much as we could so that we can help a mother have a baby. That's called prioritising, and I know it's necessary and I hate it.'

She felt she could confide in him, which was unusual for her. It was a relief to be able to say things that could not be said at the mission.

'A fortnight ago I...I had a baby die. Her mother was malnourished and weak, and the baby was premature. In England I'd have whipped her straight into an incubator—in fact, there'd have been a paediatrician and a team standing by. That baby would have survived. Here, we—well, mostly me—did what we could. But none of us is a paediatrician, and we don't have the equipment that's standard in any hospital at home. Our best wasn't good enough. The baby died. Sister O'Reilly says I shouldn't blame myself, that God only expects you to do what you can. But I felt guilty. I'm not good when babies die unnecessarily.'

Some of the anger that she so often felt must have showed itself. He reached over and stroked her arm. 'I'm sure you do do very well,' he said. 'Just remember, no doctor, no nurse, no midwife, can ever do everything. No hospital can. And worrying about it does no good.'

His words were comforting. They were what she

so often told herself—but it was good to have someone else say them.

Once again she marvelled at how she was feeling. She was sitting here, relaxed, comfortable, in a, well, a handsome man's presence. She had now decided he was handsome. Her first idea, that he was ordinary, had now disappeared. And she knew he was attracted to her.

'What brought you to Africa?' he asked, and she was alert again. This was dangerous ground, but she accepted that it was a fair question.

'I trained as a nurse first and then did my midwifery course straight away. After I'd practised a bit I decided I needed to spread my wings a bit. So I came here.' Even to herself the bald story sounded unconvincing.

He looked at her thoughtfully. 'I don't think that's all the story,' he stated flatly.

She might have guessed that he'd be sensitive enough to realise there was an awful lot she'd left unsaid. 'If it's not all the story then it's as much as I care to tell.' She knew that her voice was sharp, defensive, but there was nothing she could do about it.

Once again he reached over and stroked her bare arm. It wasn't a caress so much as an acknowledgement of their joint humanity. Still, it shocked her how much she thrilled to his touch. How could such a small thing mean so much to her?

'I didn't mean to probe,' he said. 'Forgive me.'

The best means of defence was attack. 'Tell me about yourself,' she asked. 'We see so few English doctors and it's good to hear about what is happening in England.'

'So there's no one to write to you with medical gossip?'

'My two sisters both write a lot but it's not the same as actually meeting someone.' She frowned for a moment. 'Dr Stephen James. I'm sure I've heard the name before. Dr James... Have you written any articles recently? No...what I read was by a much older man. There was a picture of him.'

He sighed. 'Gilbert James, the world-famous gynaecologist. My father, in fact.'

Gilbert James's son. What would it be like, having such a man as a father? 'I bet that was more of a handicap than an advantage when you were training,' she ventured.

He nodded. 'It was. Especially as we work in the same area. Half of my colleagues think I got my job because of my father, and the other half expect me to have his skills and knowledge. When I applied to medical school I put down that my father was a businessman. I wanted to get in on my own merits.'

'And you're still working harder than ever so you can live up to his reputation?' she probed.

He wriggled on the blanket, bringing his body just that little touch closer to hers. Apart from the scent of sun on rock, she caught the distant tang of maleness, warm and exhilarating. Why was she feeling like this?

'Yes, I suppose I've tried to live up to his reputation,' he said. 'One day I hope to surpass it. Perhaps it is a good thing.' Now their bodies were almost touching. She could sense the nearness of his flesh to hers.

He turned towards her. 'But what about you, Emily? What drives you?'

The question caught her unawares. 'Am I driven?' she managed to say. 'I'm just a midwife in Africa.'

'You're not *just* anything, Emily, and I think you *are* driven. There's something pushing you, but I don't know what.'

He was probing again, but she didn't want to tell him any more. She gave a half-truthful answer. 'I'm the middle one of three sisters. We all love each other—but perhaps I've got to prove myself more than the oldest or the youngest.' She knew there was an element of truth in this, but it wasn't the whole story.

'It often happens that way,' he agreed, but she knew he wasn't satisfied with her explanation.

They'd now finished the sandwiches and drink. There had been plenty for both—someone, indeed, did have a definite idea about how much a rugby player could eat.

At last she felt tiredness creeping up on her. It had been a long day—the early birth, then the drive and the swim. And it was so pleasant here, sitting in the shade, on the blanket. Her eyelids fluttered and closed. Just for a moment she'd…

When she woke she was half lying on him. Somehow they'd both slid down and were lying nearly flat. Her head was wonderfully comfortable on his muscled chest and shoulder as he'd stretched his arm out to cradle her. Cautiously she looked upwards—his eyes were closed, too. Good. She could lie here a while longer.

This was just not like her, she thought. Well, not like the Emily of the past three years. She was known to be tough, hard-working, ready to take charge, never vulnerable to anything. No one knew—no one was entitled to know—how she felt underneath. And yet it was good to lie here like this.

Perhaps she moved or some form of telepathy told him she was awake. His eyes opened and focussed at once. For a moment that lasted an eternity they looked at each other. Then he bent his head to kiss her.

She knew he was going to kiss her. There was a smokiness in his eyes, a fullness to his lips. She could easily have pulled away as his arm held her only lightly. But she didn't move. She wanted him to kiss her.

It was strange. She hadn't been capable of feeling physical attraction for any man so long now—well, more than two years. But there was more to it than that. This particular man excited her, and she didn't yet know why.

She sighed as his lips touched hers. She could taste the water on him and underneath the sweetness of his breath. Her body felt liquid, as if it had no power to move, all sensations gathered into one.

At first his kiss was tentative, the softest of touches. His tongue roved across her cheek to the corners of her eyes. 'I must taste like the lake,' she murmured, 'because you do.'

'You taste wonderful.' His voice was deep, caressing.

Now he kissed her lips again and under his gentle but insistent pressure she opened her mouth, wanting him. His arm tightened around her and she leaned on him more fully, taking delight in the closeness of his body to hers—feeling their skins touch and caress. She couldn't help it—her thigh splayed across his as she took his head, his body, and pulled him hard to her.

They were tight together, and all her consciousness was of his kiss. She knew what he was doing to her— even more she knew what she was doing to him. They were both excited, aroused. It was heaven!

Then she caught herself. This couldn't go on. Just a few seconds more she allowed herself, then guiltily, mournfully, she pulled herself away. He felt her hesitant movement and released her at once.

She sat up and so did he. There was only eye contact now, and she missed the warmth, the comfort, of him. 'Perhaps I should say I am sorry?' he whispered. His voice was hoarse.

She shook her head. 'Whatever happened, it was as much my fault as yours. I wanted you. But...we had to stop. Kissing is one thing, and it was lovely, but I can't give you more than that. It wouldn't be fair to you.'

He kept his body away from hers, but reached for her hand, taking it lightly. Even that touch was exquisite.

'Nothing like this ever happened to me before,' he said. 'The attraction—it was like atoms bonding.'

She saw that he was offering her a semi-comic scientific explanation as a way out of her embarrassment. But she didn't feel embarrassed. 'You mean like hydrogen and oxygen, forming water?' she asked shakily.

He took her seriously. 'Almost like that, yes. But,

if you like, we'll say it was due to the heat, the fatigue
and male and female hormones. I don't normally kiss
girls I've only just met. Even ones ás gorgeous as
you.'

He rose to his feet and offered her his hand. 'Perhaps we should go?' he said. 'Do you want to?'

There was one spark left in her. 'I don't want to,'
she said, 'but I think we should.'

They packed quickly and expertly. She told him not
to follow her too closely as her dust would make driving difficult. It was only an hour and a half's drive to
the mission so they would arrive in time for afternoon
tea. She was the old, efficient Emily Grey again. Just
before they climbed into their vehicles Stephen kissed
her again.

'Was it only heat, tiredness and hormones between
us?' he asked softly.

She was honest. 'No,' she said. 'I don't know what
it was. It was like nothing I've ever experienced before. But I think we'd better forget it.'

'That would be hard,' he said.

She couldn't reply. She climbed up into her Land
Rover. She knew it would be hard for her, too.

It was good to have something different to concentrate on. The rough path down from the pool took all
her attention. But once on the main road driving was
easier and she had time to think. In her rear-view mirror she could see the new Land Rover behind, and
found herself glancing at it constantly.

She thought about the kiss, and why her insides
were churning with a heady excitement. Dr Stephen
James was exciting. And she hadn't been excited this
way for so long. She hadn't been capable of being

excited by a man. She told herself to forget him.
Feelings like this led only to misery. And she hardly
knew him.

The two vehicles pulled up outside St Winefride's
Mission Hospital. As ever, when returning after a trip,
Emily felt a thrill. This was a place where she had
worked harder than ever before and had found a life
which was testing but satisfying. It was a place where,
when she'd thought she'd never be happy again, she
had found some happiness.

The main hospital was built of cement blocks, with
corrugated iron roofing. The glassless windows were
shuttered and fitted with insect screens. Inside were
old iron bedsteads with straw mattresses that could
easily be burned in case of infection. In the back-
ground could be heard the rattle of the generator. The
hospital was simple, primitive even, but it saved lives
and cured illnesses. She loved it.

Sister O'Reilly came down the wooden steps to
welcome them, obviously thinking that they had arrived together coincidentally. Emily spoke first, explaining how she'd already met Dr James in a stolen
hour by the pool.

As ever, Sister's face gave nothing away, but Emily
knew her apparently guileless brown eyes hid a keen
and sometimes cunning brain.

'Both of you go for a shower,' she said. 'You look
as though you need it. Then, Dr James, I'd like to
introduce you to the rest of the staff. I'm sorry Dr
Mugumo isn't here. He was called away this morning
to an accident, but leaves his apologies. Perhaps we
could all have a cup of tea in twenty minutes?'

'That would be nice,' he said gravely.

'Then I'll take you to your room.'

He collected his bag from the back of the Land Rover and the three of them walked to the tiny bungalows that were the staff quarters. 'How is Eunice coping?' Sister asked Emily when Stephen had disappeared into his room. 'Are you happy about leaving her behind?'

'Quite happy,' Emily said decisively. 'She's good at what she knows and she's not getting over-confident. Another year or so and she'll be a very competent midwife.'

'That's good to hear. The sooner we get local staff trained the sooner we can go home, Emily.'

Emily smiled. This was a frequent remark—and one which everyone ignored. 'You love it here,' she said.

'Perhaps I do. But sometimes I miss the soft rain.'

'The mission offered you the chance of a break in Ireland a year ago,' Emily teased. 'You told then you'd stay here and they could spend the money on a set of cots.'

Sister sniffed. 'I wasn't ready for a holiday. And I had work to do.' She decided that was enough sentiment. 'There again, I like the sun here. Tea in twenty minutes. I want you there when we talk to Dr James.'

'I thought I'd just nip down to the ward and check on my patients,' Emily said. 'I've not—'

'Your patients are fine. Other people are looking after them.' Sister fumbled in her pocket. 'But there is one thing, a letter from Sally M'Bono. She went home yesterday with baby Solomon—both doing fine.'

Emily read the letter, laboriously printed on a piece of paper taken from an exercise book. Sally thanked Emily for what she had done, and said the next baby girl but one would be called Emily.

'Next girl but one?' queried Emily, showing Sister the letter.

'Mother-in-law comes first,' Sister said practically. 'Some things are the same in Africa as they are in Ireland.'

'It cheers me up to get a letter like this,' Emily said. 'Makes it all worthwhile.'

'Makes me wonder what they're doing at the mission school,' Sister said. 'It took Sally far too long to finish that letter. Now, if I were in charge—'

'Don't tell me you want to be a teacher as well as a nurse!'

'Well, I made my choice when I was young. Now, off you go and I'll see you in twenty minutes.' Sister had made her wishes known, and they would be obeyed.

Emily entered her bare little room. There were no pictures on the walls, no flowers or ornaments. Only an old photograph of her with her father and her two sisters, and a more recent one of her sister, Lisa, getting married. She had decided not to fly home for the ceremony. Now she was regretting her decision.

First she showered, rinsing the smell of the pool out of her hair and from her body. Then, instead of her customary shorts and shirt, she put on a dress. It was made of a patterned blue and white linen, and it set off her tan. It hung from her, now too big. Yet she remembered it fitting perfectly. Shrugging, she pulled in the belt an extra notch.

Drinking tea out on the verandah was pleasant. It almost seemed as if they were playing parts, pretending to be rich visitors passing through the country and being idly curious about it. For once the flies and the insects weren't being a nuisance. Unfortunately, Sam wasn't back yet, but Sister had fetched a number of the staff who weren't working and they sat on the edges of their seats, decorously sipping from their cups as if this was the way they behaved every day.

Sister was at her most bland, sitting by Stephen on the wooden couch and smiling at him amiably. She waved a letter. 'It was good of you to deliver our new Land Rover,' she said. 'It saved Joseph a trip out to fetch it.' Joseph was their driver, mechanic and general handyman. Sister went on, 'I gather you're just here to look round—see how we do things away from civilisation. And we're very pleased to have you. You're not here to work—you must have a little holiday. But…if there's an odd query, I'm sure you'll offer advice.'

Emily watched Stephen's expression remain calm and polite. 'I'll be happy to offer what help I can,' he said, 'and I'm looking forward to visiting the wards.'

Hastily Sister finished her tea. 'In that case,' she said, 'I'll just see what might—uh—interest you. Don't get up. I'll just run down to see that everything is ready for you.'

But, of course, Stephen did stand up, and Emily winked at him. The fish had taken the bait. Unfortunately Sister had seen the wink, and adopted the other-worldly expression that meant she was plotting. 'Of course, Emily here is in charge of the gynaecological ward,' she said. 'That'll obviously be your particular interest. We'll visit them last. I'm sure she'd love to show you round.'

Another hint, and not a small one. 'I'll go to the ward at once,' Emily said.

Stephen laid his hand on her arm. 'You haven't drunk your tea,' he said, 'and Sister needs a few minutes first. You can tell me more about the work here.'

Sister looked approving. 'Come down in fifteen minutes,' she said.

Emily changed into her uniform—such as it was—and marshalled the staff, telling them they were expecting an important visitor. Then she waited for Sister and Stephen.

There were ten beds in Emily's little ward, all occupied. Six were, she hoped, to be straightforward births. The other four had problems.

From somewhere Sister had found Stephen a white coat. The rest of his outfit might be casual, but the coat and the stethoscope round his neck made him look the doctor he so obviously was. His manner, too, had changed. Emily's heart bumped. She couldn't have said why, but there was something about his tone, the way he looked at her patients, that indicated he was an expert in his field.

There was now no pretence about him just being shown round. He looked hard at the medical records and asked Emily searching questions about her patients. But he also had time to smile at the patients, and chat to two who spoke English. He asked to examine the four with problems.

Afterwards there was a meeting in her tiny ward

office. Sister had asked that as many trainees as possible be present. They needed to learn.

'I am not the doctor here,' he said, 'and in no way am I going to prescribe treatment. To begin with, I shall shortly be gone. These are Dr Mugumo's patients and I've no wish to interfere with his treatment. However, Sister here suggests he will have no objection if I talk about some of his cases.'

He's a good teacher, Emily thought as he stepped up to her blackboard. Now, why am I not surprised at that? From bitter experience she knew that good clinical teachers were rare.

'There are four cases here that give cause for concern,' he went on, 'a case of hypertension, also known as pre-eclampsia, a case of gestational diabetes, a simple unstable lie and a lady who has been hospitalised because of early ruptured membranes. Now, take the first…'

It was a good lesson. After the trainees had gone there was another meeting, just Stephen, Sister and herself, in which he delicately suggested possible variations or alternative treatments. Emily felt a lot happier about a couple of the cases now she'd had his expert opinion. She knew Sam wouldn't mind Stephen's advice in the least.

It was dark when they left the ward. Sister looked suitably surprised. 'Look at the time we've been,' she said. 'And you're supposed to be on holiday, Dr James. You will tell us if we're working you too hard, won't you?'

'Of course,' he agreed urbanely. To Emily he managed to whisper, 'If I dare, that is.' Somehow she kept a straight face.

* * *

Emily went to bed, not knowing how she was feeling—only that she was tired. Stephen had made an impression on her, but she didn't have the strength to decide what kind of impression it was. She thought she'd have a minute to reflect on the day. But the moment her eyes closed she slept.

As happened so often, she was woken in the middle of the night. The duty nurse tapped on her door, then came in and shook her firmly. 'Sorry, Mis' Grey, but we got an emergency. Just been brought in by the oxcart. Been in labour for twenty-four hours now.'

Emily rubbed her head. She'd been having a marvellous dream, she was sure. But now it was gone, and reality was intruding. And she was still tired. 'All right, Anna, I'll be there straight away.'

Quickly she filled her basin with cold water and dipped her head into it. It was a shock but it had the necessary effect. She was awake. It took her little time to dress and she walked rapidly to the room they used as a delivery suite. Once there it was easy to make a decision. This was more than a slow baby. It would have to be born by Caesarean section.

In the past she'd helped to perform the operation with Sam, but Sam still wasn't back. Stephen James was here, however, and she couldn't attempt the operation herself. She explained to the orderly and the two trainee midwives what was needed to prep the mother, then did her best to reassure the terrified young girl. Then she slipped back to the residential block.

She wasn't surprised to see Sister O'Reilly, waiting there. Sister had a sixth sense about emergencies. 'You need your sleep, Emily. Why are you up?'

Emily explained. 'A girl's just come in in labour. I think she's going to need a Caesarean and I'm going to ask Dr James to help.'

'Good idea. He'll do better than either of us could.'

'What happens if he needs his sleep, too?' Emily asked with a grin.

'Well, the choice is his. That's why you can wake him and not me.'

In the dark Emily blinked. At times Sister O'Reilly could be forthright. 'You go back to bed,' Emily said. 'No need for everyone to be tired out.'

'If I'm needed...'

'If you're needed we'll be banging on the door.'

Sister O'Reilly went. She knew things were under control.

Outside Stephen's door Emily felt a momentary qualm. She stifled it. There was work to be done. She rapped loudly on the door then opened it. The rooms were small so the bed was at once obvious. He stirred and sat up under the sheet. His naked body gleamed in the half-light. For a moment she shivered with an anticipation that had nothing to do with medical matters.

'Is that Emily?' His voice was warm, still slurred with sleep.

'Dr James—Stephen—we've got an emergency and I don't know if I can cope.'

He'd obviously been woken in the night many times in the past. Instantly his voice became alert. 'Give me two minutes and I'll be there. Where are you?'

'Next to the operating theatre. I think we'll have to perform a Caesarean.' She hurried back to her patient.

He was with her as quickly as he'd said, clad solely
in shorts and singlet. Somehow he'd learned the name
of the patient, and he leaned over her, smiling, and
said, 'It's Matilda, isn't it? Well, Matilda, let's see if
we can sort this baby out.' His ease, his obvious com-
petence, made everyone there feel easier at once.

His examination was quickly over. He motioned
Emily to follow him and muttered, 'You're right, we
need a Caesarean. I'm not happy about the baby's
heart rate—it's too low for my liking. What kit have
you got ready?'

'Well, we haven't got an anaesthetist so it'll have
to be an epidural anaesthetic. I've got a Tuohy needle
ready and the catheter is here. Is that what you want?'

'I'm happy with that.'

'Otherwise, I think we've got all you will need.
Sam and I did a section last month. I'm quite used to
being scrub nurse.'

'I think you'll be good at it. Come on, show me
the kit and then we'll scrub up.'

CHAPTER THREE

THE operation went perfectly. Stephen was a model surgeon—patient, careful—involving those around him in what he was doing. Matilda, the mother, was obviously terrified. She'd never been in an operating theatre before, but she seemed to respond to Stephen's calm words and reassuring manner.

The baby was born without undue trouble, and passed to a trainee who showed him to the mother. The section was patiently sutured and mother and baby were wheeled into Emily's ward, where another bed had been crammed in. There was nothing else that could be done now. Although Emily wanted to stay, she knew it was foolish. The trainee midwife was quite capable of looking after the mother and baby Aaron. He now had a fighting chance.

Emily made the trainee repeat her instructions. 'Don't forget, Rachel,' she said. 'Any problem, you are to wake me. I don't mind at all. You understand?'

'Yes, miss. I wake you if necessary.'

'Good.' She turned to Stephen. 'Would you like a cup of tea before you go back to bed?' she asked. 'And I'm sorry we had to disturb you when you're not even working here.'

He smiled. 'I would have been very angry if you hadn't woken me. And I'd had a sleep already.' He accepted the cup she handed him, and then said, 'But you look tired, Emily.'

She felt tired. It was normal. 'I've had a long day,' she said.

He rubbed his lips with his finger. 'It's more than that—you're deep-down tired. I think you've been working too hard for months. You need a rest.'

He was intruding. She snapped back at him. 'Didn't you work long, tiring hours when you were studying? Don't you still?'

He was unmoved by her attack. 'Yes,' he agreed, 'I work hard and I always have. But once I really overdid it and I made a mistake. Not a big one, but one caused by fatigue.' He sipped his tea. 'A tired nurse is a bad nurse, Emily. You know that.'

'A bad, tired nurse is better than no nurse at all.' She gulped down her tea. 'D'you want to go back to bed now?' She led him silently back to the residential block.

Just before she said goodnight to him it struck her that she was being unfair. This man was supposed to be a guest and she'd dragged him out of bed and made him work. He'd helped willingly.

'I'm sorry if I sounded sharp,' she said. 'I really am most grateful for what you've done. And...you might be right. I could be overtired. Will you forgive me?'

'There's nothing to forgive, Emily. Goodnight.' His voice was soft, almost loving. They'd stopped outside his door. She wondered if he would... But he touched her once on the arm and stepped inside.

He didn't go back to bed at once. He undressed, looked round his spartan room and peered through the shuttered window at the bright-starred African sky. So different from the mild skies of England. He wasn't

sleepy. Something was bothering him. He lay on the
bed, his hands behind his head, and thought.

Why was he so happy that Emily had turned him
out of bed at three in the morning? Why was he so
pleased to do something to help her—something, he
knew, that would make her think better of him? He
wanted her good opinion.

Perhaps she was too thin. But there was strength in
that lean body, and beauty, too. There was strength
and beauty in her face—but he thought he could detect signs of a softer person under that iron self-
sufficiency.

There had been women in his life before, of course,
but never one he'd reacted to so quickly. He recalled
that magic vision of her, walking wet from the pool.
She had been both proud and vulnerable. And so
beautiful. He sighed. He wanted to see more of midwife Emily Grey, but he suspected it wouldn't be in
the next few days.

As Emily had guessed, Stephen didn't get much of a
holiday. It was never quiet at St Winefride's Mission
Hospital, but sometimes it was busier than normal. A
trainee midwife and two of the auxilliary nurses fell
ill, several cases of tuberculosis were suddenly discovered in a nearby village and for some reason there
were more difficult births than normal. Any suggestion that Stephen might be at the hospital for a rest
mysteriously disappeared, and he worked willingly,
helping Emily and the overworked Sam.

Emily could think of nothing but the tasks ahead
of her. Only occasionally, perhaps when they were
snatching a cup of tea together, did she remember that

kiss by the lake. And it seemed to her that he, too, hadn't forgotten what had happened. Once or twice she caught him looking at her in a way that made her feel both uncomfortable and excited.

He didn't try to kiss her again. They were alone occasionally but, for some reason they both silently acknowledged, the mission wasn't the right place. And they never got out of the mission. But she thought about him, kissing her, and came to no firm conclusion.

Stephen had driven the Land Rover from Golanda, the nearest large town, some two hundred miles away. He'd arrived on Tuesday afternoon and the original intention had been that Joseph should drive him back very early on Saturday morning. There was a plane that left Golanda airport late every afternoon, where he could catch a flight back to Johannesburg five hundred miles away.

On Friday afternoon an already difficult week suddenly got even worse. Word came through of an accident sixty miles away. It was the kind of emergency the mission had dealt with in the past. One of the old, unreliable lorries, which were used as people transporters, had rolled over and slid down a ravine, killing two people and injuring many more.

Sister, Sam and two auxiliaries would take two of the Land Rovers, packed with medical supplies, and set up a temporary clinic at the nearest village. They would be away for two or three days. Emily would be left in charge with the last Land Rover.

'I'll stay an extra day,' Stephen said as he and Emily waved goodbye to the departing vehicles. 'If I set off early on Sunday morning I'll still be able to catch a plane back in time for my match.'

'That's good of you,' Emily said.' 'We certainly need the extra help.' There was a tiny throb of excitement at the thought of being with Stephen. However, it was soon suppressed—there was work to do. 'Would you like to take Sam's evening round?' she asked.

Saturday was hard, too, but Emily was always conscious that, if only for a while, she and Stephen were in charge of the mission. It gave her a feeling of togetherness, of complicity even. She knew he had to go, and would probably disappear from her life for ever. But that was in the future—she would concentrate on her life in the present.

At six that evening all her feelings of warmth, of togetherness, were blown apart.

It started with a message from Eunice who had been in the distant village of Kulimamo. A man turned up on an ancient bicycle with a letter. Serwalo, the woman who was expected to give birth in three or four weeks, was being brought slowly to the mission. She would arrive at about midday tomorrow.

In a detailed letter, Eunice explained that Serwalo had had a sudden severe haemorrhage. The blood was bright red. Although very anxious, Serwalo appeared to be in no pain and there was no pain felt when the abdomen was palpated. However, her blood pressure was low and her pulse rate raised. She hoped she was doing right in bringing Serwalo to the mission.

Emily reread the letter and sat down to think. Certainly Eunice was doing the right thing in bringing Serwalo here. There were other causes of bleeding,

but it sounded as if Serwalo was suffering from placenta praevia. The placenta had attached too low in
the uterus and might even be blocking the internal
cervical os. There was no way out for the baby—
except by Caesarean section.

She had helped Sam with Caesarean sections before
and, of course, she'd been with Stephen when he'd
performed one a few nights ago. But Sam wasn't here
and Stephen was leaving. She couldn't perform such
an operation alone, but Stephen could—she'd ask him
to put off his departure for another day.

She asked him over their evening meal. So far he'd
been relaxed and casual, apparently taking pleasure in
her company. He'd chatted easily about his training
in London. She, on the other hand, felt on edge, and
knew it showed in her manner. Later, when they sat
side by side on the verandah, he asked her why.
'Something's bothering you, Emily. Want to tell me
what it is?'

Yes, she did want to tell him, but she was terrified
of what his answer might be.

'I've got a woman coming in with what I think
might be placenta praevia,' she said. 'She won't arrive
until about twelve tomorrow and I think she'll need a
Caesarean. I was wondering...if you'll stay behind
and do it.'

He seemed genuinely regretful. 'You know I can't,
Emily,' he said sadly. 'This match I'm to play in is
important and I've already stayed here too long.'

'Isn't a woman's baby more important than your
rugby match?' She could see he was disturbed, even
angered by her harsh tones. But he still answered patiently.

'Of course a baby's life is more important but decisions have to be made, Emily. If I stay one extra day to help this woman, then should I stay the next day to help someone else? And then another day? Why not stay here for my entire vacation? But other people are counting on me and I feel I have to stick to my schedule. Remember how you told me how hard it was to prioritise? Well, this is another example of it. Now, what we can do is go through the problem and if there's any advice I can offer you I will.'

'I don't want your advice. I want your skill. I want you physically present in that operating theatre.'

She'd said it and he was angry. 'Emily, I'm leaving here early tomorrow morning. Until then you can have all my time, all my skill. But I must be on that plane. Other people depend on me and I've stayed here too long already.'

'And that's your last word?'

'Positively my last word. I'm sorry.'

'I see.' She slammed her cup down in her saucer. 'If you'll excuse me, I've got patients I want to see. Do finish your tea.' She walked rapidly off the verandah, not trusting herself to stay with him longer. Who cared about his rugby match, anyway?

This was not the way she'd intended to spend her last day with Stephen. She'd wanted something more friendly, more intimate. But her patients had to come first. She would go back and ask him what advice he could give her. Perhaps she could cope. Perhaps Sam would be back in time. And, again, perhaps neither of these would happen. She was a midwife, not a gynaecologist.

Often, when she was upset, she'd go into her ward

to peer at the babies she'd helped to be born. It calmed her to see how something she was doing here was successful. And the sight of those little breathing bodies aroused in her thoughts that she did not like to enquire into. She only knew they were comforting.

It was while she was looking at four-day-old Aaron, born weighing only three pounds but clinging vigorously to life, that the idea came to her. At first she rejected it out of hand, but it wouldn't go away. Why not? she asked herself.

Stephen expected Joseph to drive him in the Land Rover to Golanda early tomorrow morning. They were to leave at six. Without the Land Rover there was no way Stephen could leave the mission. There was no other vehicle within a radius of fifty miles. If Emily sent Joseph away with the Land Rover, Stephen would have to stay. And if he stayed here he'd perform the operation—help Serwalo. She knew he would. He'd have to.

She couldn't bear to see him again that evening. Instead, she sent an auxiliary to say that she'd gone to bed early and that they'd meet in the morning.

It was rare for her not to sleep the minute she climbed into bed, but tonight she was restless. Plans, fears, worries, tormented her. Then, in the most desolate hour of the night, she woke. She switched on her bedside light and looked round her bare room at the pictures of her family, seeking guidance from somewhere.

There was something she was not admitting to herself. She was attracted to Stephen. He had affected her more than anyone had done for a long, long time.

He had aroused feelings in her that she'd thought had
gone for good.

And she thought he might feel something for her,
too. She was sure that after he'd left he'd be in touch
with her some way or another. They'd meet again.

But she now knew his character. He would listen
to any argument but he was sturdily independent.
He'd make up his own mind. If she crossed him she
knew that any feeling he had for her would disappear.
The choice was stark. Should she think of her own
forlorn hope of happiness or the life of a child? She
made up her mind. She would do it. Then she slept.

The air was cool first thing in the morning. Usually
this was the time that Emily enjoyed most. But not
today. She rose early, before Stephen would be
awake, and gave Joseph his instructions. He was to
take supplies to a village some fifty miles away,
which she was due to visit in a week. There was no
way he'd be back before evening. She listened to the
roar of the engine, dying away, then went to find
Stephen. There was no turning back now.

He'd already packed and she shivered as she saw
his two cases on the verandah steps. He was sitting
inside at the breakfast table, drinking tea. She didn't
know how to tell him. In his shorts and white shirt
he looked, well, kissable. What a thing to think now!

He stood and smiled tentatively as she approached.
'Emily, I'll be going soon and I'd hate it if we weren't
friends when we parted. Can we patch up our differences somehow?'

She slumped into a seat opposite him. She hadn't
thought it possible to feel worse, but she did. 'No, I

don't think we can patch up our differences,' she said. 'You don't know what I've done.'

His expression was curious. 'What have you done?' he asked.

There was no easy way of telling him, no way to avert his anger. She'd have to tell him boldly. 'I've sent Joseph away with the only Land Rover. He won't be back till late this evening.'

'You've done what?' He obviously hadn't realised what this meant.

'I've made sure that you can't leave this mission for the next ten hours.'

She wouldn't have thought it possible for a face to change so completely. The smiling, engaging expression was replaced by a bleak, iron-hard mask. 'I thought I had explained that it was imperative that I arrive in Johannesburg by tomorrow.'

'You did. But I wanted… I'm sorry.' She could feel her voice quavering.

He must have thought that she hadn't meant what she'd said, that there was some way she could conjure up another vehicle. 'I don't want you to feel sorry. I want you to arrange for me to get to Golanda by early this afternoon. Good Lord, woman, there must be another vehicle somewhere near here!'

'There isn't. Not even a tractor. Have you seen one in the past few days?'

Full realisation was dawning now. 'You mean I'm trapped here? There's no possible way of leaving?' When he got angry his voice didn't rise. If anything, it got softer, but the menace in it was obvious.

He still hadn't fully grasped what she had done. With what was obviously a great effort, he managed to ask calmly, 'Emily, why couldn't Joseph take me, as well as running this errand for you? Or couldn't his trip have waited another day?'

She would have to face his full anger. 'There was no important errand for Joseph. I sent him away so you would have to stay and operate on Serwalo.'

His voice was now so soft as to be almost a whisper. 'I have to get back to Johannesburg. How dare you make decisions for me?'

From somewhere she summoned the strength to fight back. 'Serwalo needs to have this baby. Only you can manage it so you have to stay. I'm sorry if it's messed up your rugby match, but I still think she's more important.'

'What d'you think I am?' His icy voice lashed at her like a whip. 'D'you think it's the kind of decision I take lightly? D'you think I liked leaving her behind? There are facts you know nothing of, but you still happily made *my* decision. I find your arrogance beyond belief. Midwives are important, but doctors make decisions. Now I'm going to find some way of getting out of this God-forsaken hole and driving back to Golanda.'

'This isn't a God-forsaken hole,' she said quietly, 'and I assure you that there is no way of leaving it till Joseph gets back. You're stuck here, Dr James. And it's all my fault. It was my decision. Take your anger out on me, not on the workers here.'

He walked around the table and, half-afraid, she rose to meet him. He grabbed her by the arms and a distant part of her mind registered the pain his grip was causing her. She could feel the tears blurring her vision as she peered into the incandescent fury of his eyes.

'You think too much of yourself and your right to decide,' he snarled.

She shook her head. 'I think nothing of myself, but I do think of my patients.' It was feeble defiance, but all that she could manage.

'I just don't want to look at you.' Contemptuously he pushed her away from him so that she lost her balance and sat back in an undignified heap on the cane chair behind her. 'I'm going to make sure you're telling the truth. I certainly won't take your word.'

The door slammed behind him. Emily sat, her tears dropping onto the wooden floor.

There was still work for her to do. Somehow she managed to oversee all the little jobs that needed her decisions for the next two hours. Fortunately, nothing too crucial occurred. She could tell that the trainees and auxiliaries were curious but she said nothing. She gathered that Stephen had walked around the little compound, asking if there were any vehicles nearby. The answer had always been no. He hadn't bullied or shouted at the staff. But, then, she'd known that would be the case.

His bags remained as a reproof on the verandah steps. There was no work for him to do as Emily had arranged a rota on the previous day. He went back to his room and remained there.

Just after midday Serwalo arrived, lying on the back of a cart pulled by two oxen. Eunice was with her, looking worried. They had made good time. Emily hadn't expected them for another four hours. Hastily she inspected the woman.

It was as Eunice had said. Sewalo had lost much blood. Emily ordered a plasma expander and for Serwalo's blood to be typed. Serwalo's pulse was rapid and her skin felt clammy, but her temperature was normal. There was no infection. Quickly using her Pinard stethoscope, Emily listened to the baby's heart. It was still beating, but not strongly.

Emily was sure now that this was a case of placenta praevia. She ordered Serwalo to be prepped and taken to the little theatre then she went to Stephen's room and knocked loudly on the door.

He certainly hadn't forgiven her. His face was teak-hard as he stared at her. She swallowed her fear and attacked at once.

'Serwalo has just arrived. I'm having her prepped and sent to the theatre. I'm pretty sure it's placenta praevia, type three or even type four. Are you going to take your anger out on her and refuse to operate? If so, I'll have to.'

He held out his hands in front of her. 'Look,' he said harshly, 'my hands are still shaking. With fury. How would it be if I made a mistake? Whose fault would it be then?'

For Emily the answer was clear. 'You're a doctor,' she said flatly. 'At the moment you're not allowed personal feelings. Now, will you be over in fifteen minutes?'

The silence between them couldn't have been long, but for her it seemed to stretch for ever.

'I'll come over now,' he said.

She couldn't let herself falter, not at this late stage. But how she wished she'd made a different decision. He looked at her as if he hated her.

*　　*　　*

Obviously he wanted to examine Serwalo, before carrying out any kind of operation. Emily was impressed by the way he smiled at her and reassured her, explaining exactly what he was doing and how he hoped everything would go well. The terrified woman spoke some English and responded to his kindness, relaxing as best she could. To the auxiliaries, too, he was courteous, remembering that they could only learn if they took every opportunity to observe.

Only to her was he formal, curt in his instructions. Well, she deserved it.

The Caesarean section was a success. Emily was fascinated to watch his skill, to see the way he became absorbed in his work. The baby was small but viable, and should survive. Emily saw him into the care of the trainee midwives, and then returned to assist Stephen. Finally he was finished and, with a last few words to the watchers, Serwalo was carefully wheeled back into the ward.

'I'll get you a drink,' Emily said as they pulled off their gowns. 'I think you need one.'

'Thank you. But first I'll dictate some notes about nursing. I wouldn't want my work to be spoiled by careless aftercare.'

Emily flinched. 'I'll take that insult. I suppose you're entitled. But it's unworthy of you. Tell me, could either I or Sam have performed that operation as well as you?'

He hesitated. 'No,' he said, with reluctant honesty.

'I'm glad I didn't have to try. Just remember, because of what you've done that woman has a son and can now have more babies.'

'I know that. I've never been in any doubt about it.'

'Come over for your tea,' she mumbled. She'd made her decision much earlier, and she still believed it was right. But more and more she was regretting it.

They sat in hostile silence, drinking the tea that had been brought to them. She was beginning to feel the beginnings of a headache. It must be guilt because she never had headaches. When he spoke to her she thought she had been partly forgiven, but it turned out that his rage had changed to a cold anger which she found even harder to take.

'What you did was unforgivable. If you'd done anything like it in England, I'd ensure that you never practised again.'

She felt weak under the bleakness of his gaze. He went on, 'I didn't just come here on a sporting jamboree. My trip was sponsored by a charity that has organised a number of rugby matches. As you know, the sport is very popular here. We paid for our own tickets. The money raised by the matches was to finance a new children's ward in a hospital in this country.

'I've now let down that charity, and I feel very badly about it. Not to be arrogant, but I know quite a few people would have turned out just to see me play. I have something of a reputation. I don't like letting them down.'

She faltered, 'You could tell them that I—'

'There is nothing that I could tell them. I certainly won't try. The facts are obvious, I went for a short holiday and couldn't be bothered to get back in time. Please tell me the minute the Land Rover arrives. I'll drive. Joseph can come with me and drive back.' He went back to his room.

Perhaps Joseph had misunderstood her directions, perhaps subconsciously she hadn't wanted him to stay away all day. Anyway, he came back early. Emily made the arrangements, gave orders for Stephen to be called and had his bags placed in the back of the vehicle. Then she waited in the little common room. He was entitled to see her on her own to say goodbye and insult her for the last time. She was not going to hide behind the protective cover of the others in the compound.

He didn't seem to have mellowed. 'I'll set off now. Six hours too late. So there's no chance of my catching the plane. I shall miss tomorrow's game.'

She seemed to have done nothing else but apologise all day. 'For what it's worth, I'm sorry.' And she was. She was beginning to realise that she'd done something not only unprofessional but also unfair. He was entitled to be angry with her.

'*Are* you sorry? I suspect you'd do exactly the same again if you thought it necessary. Wouldn't you?' The words were snarled, but he seemed to expect an answer.

'Probably,' she croaked. 'I...I've put sandwiches and a drink in the Land Rover.'

By the way he looked at her she knew he was remembering how they had shared his sandwiches—was it only five days before? She coloured at the memory. What must he think of her now? 'Thank you,' he said ironically, 'I've been worrying in case I didn't have enough to eat.'

He had been standing just inside the door. Now he

shut it with a crash and came towards her. She forced herself not to back away. 'I'll go now. And thank God I'll never have to see you again.'

He took her shoulders in his hands and pulled her towards him. His kiss was brutal—an assault, not a caress. His tongue forced open her mouth and his strong arms crushed her to him. She didn't fight back, but wrapped her hands lightly behind him. She felt she was being punished, but some part of her knew that she liked it. Finally he pushed her away.

For a moment she looked at him, then leaned forward and kissed him on the cheek. 'Thank you for what you've done for the mission,' she said. 'And for what you've done for me.'

'Goodbye!' The door slammed again as he strode out. She hadn't the strength to follow him. She heard the roar of the Land Rover engine and knew he was driving—too fast. She hoped he'd be safe.

The headache she'd felt starting earlier had now got worse. She'd love to sit here and nurse her problems, but she was in charge of the mission and had work to do. Forcing herself to stand, she went to check on Serwalo.

The fight with Stephen must have taken more out of her than she had thought. Halfway through the afternoon she had to go back to the common room and sit for half an hour because she felt so dreadful. She would have lain down in her room, but she'd never done that in the middle of the day.

She lapsed into a half-doze. Then she heard the sound of engines. Making herself stand, she went to the door. Coming up the track were two Land Rovers.

Sam, Sister and the others were back early. She had never been so pleased to see anyone before.

Sam went straight to his room and said he'd have a look round the wards after a shower. Sister said she'd have a cup of tea and talk to Emily. Emily looked at her, surprised. How did Sister know that she had something to confess?

Emily sat there as Sister ran round, organising the tea and chatting about the accident they'd attended. It turned out that things hadn't been quite as bad as had been expected. They'd been useful but not vitally necessary, which was why they'd come back early. Finally the two of them were sitting together on the couch, the ever-welcome tea in hand.

'I've got a confession to make,' Emily said baldly, and told Sister what she'd done. She didn't try to excuse herself, and was particular in reporting Stephen's justified anger.

'How is Serwalo?' Sister asked before anything else.

'She's doing fine and so is the baby. Stephen—Dr James—is a very good doctor. I couldn't have done what he did.'

'So some good has come of things. But it's a poor way we've repaid the man's kindness in working so hard for us while he was here.'

'I know that. What would you have done, Sister?'

Unusually for her, Sister leaned forward and rested her hands on top of Emily's. 'Well, I'd like to think that at your young age I'd have done the same as you, Emily. I used to think that everything was black and white, and what was right was obvious. But I'm afraid you weren't right. People must make their own decisions. I think you know that. Now, give me your wrist.'

To Emily's amazement she found her pulse being taken.

'I thought so. You go straight to bed and I'll bring Sam to see you in five minutes.'

'But I've got my work—'

'Someone else will do it. You're part of the work now, Emily. You're ill.'

'But I've got to—'

'No one is indispensable. And the way you look now, you'd be a hindrance not a help to any ward. We'll cope without you. Now, off you go.'

She didn't want an argument. She went.

Next morning she knew Sister had been right. She felt dreadful. She was told she'd have to stay in bed a few days longer. She tried to get up and fell flat on the floor.

'You are ill,' Sister said severely, helping her back. 'Now, being ill is no sin, but thinking that only you can do certain things is certainly approaching one. It's pride. You must rest.'

'What's wrong with me?' Emily asked thickly.

Sister looked worried. She fetched a mirror and made Emily look at her eyes. They were noticeably yellow. 'Have you had a needlestick in the past few months?'

No matter how hard nurses tried, every now and again they would stab themselves with an unsterile needle. It was a hazard of the job. 'One or two, I suppose,' Emily said.

'Well, at a guess I'd say you have got hepatitis. You're looking jaundiced, but it doesn't show so much under your tan. The worst news would be that it's hepatitis B. I hope not. I'll take some blood and we'll look at it. Anyway, we're shipping you off to the hospital in Golanda. They can deal with you more easily than we can.'

'I don't want hepatitis B,' Emily cried, appalled. 'I could never be a midwife again.'

'I know. Now it's all in the good Lord's hands, and we'll know more later. Try to rest.'

Emily didn't have the strength to argue. Suddenly her world had shifted, become uncertain. Hepatitis B was blood-carried. If she had it she would never again be able to work in a hospital. Certainly she would never again be able to perform the invasive tasks that midwifery so often demanded.

'When will I be able to come back, Sister? *Will* I be able to come back?'

Sister sighed. 'I don't think you will be coming back, Emily. Your contract will be up in a couple of weeks. There's already a replacement for you on her way. Your time here is ended and you must go back and rejoin your own. You have to stop hiding.'

'Hiding from what?' Emily tried to be angry but found she just didn't have the strength.

'I don't know what you're hiding from but I know you're hiding from something. I had my doubts about you when you came. Too many people come out here more concerned about their own problems than those they're supposed to be looking after. Usually they crawl back in a month or two. But you've done well. Now go back and start living again.'

For some reason Emily hadn't thought about her

contract coming to an end. She'd not thought of the future at all. There was only the ever-present work.

'But there's my work...' she muttered.

'It'll be done,' Sister said gently. 'Now stop worrying and get well.'

A week later Emily was driven down to the hospital in Golanda in the new Land Rover, which could be converted into a semi-ambulance. Sister came with her. It wasn't the kind of leave-taking she'd envisaged. In fact, she'd never thought of leaving at all. She'd made no plans, being content merely to deal with the problems of the day, but now she was saying goodbye to people she'd come to know and love over the past two years.

The journey was a nightmare, and she was glad when she was assisted into bed in the strangely modern-looking ward. Sister, of course, had to go straight back, but she made Emily promise to keep in touch. Emily sighed as she left. Now she could relax and let others look after her, as she had looked after so many.

She was diagnosed as suffering from Hepatitis A. When cured, she would be able to work in hospital again. Upon being told, she merely shook her head, indifferent to the good news. Her condition was made worse by the fact that she was near exhaustion. She stayed in the hospital for three weeks, spent in a near coma, before being put on the plane to Johannesburg. Then there was another stay, this time in an international, state-of-the-art hospital.

Finally she flew halfway across the world to Manchester. She was coming home. Waiting for her were two girls with hair as red as her own—her sis-

ters, Lisa and Rosalind. Emily broke down in tears.
She hadn't realised how much she'd missed them.

'What have you been doing to yourself?' Lisa
asked, equally tearful.

'You need feeding up,' Rosalind said. 'Welcome home.'

CHAPTER FOUR

NONE of the family put in a word for Emily but it
wasn't too long before she had a new job. It was all
right to do nothing while she was ill. But she was
now getting better.

For a while she was staying with her sister, Lisa,
and her new brother-in-law, Alex. She liked Alex, she
liked his children, Holly and Jack, from his first marriage and she liked his mother, Lucy, who still kept
an eye on the children. It appeared to be an idyllic
marriage, and Emily felt very happy for Lisa and just
the tiniest touch envious.

Then, after a fortnight, when the two sisters were
sitting in the kitchen, Lisa put a paper in front of her.
Blazes, the hospital where both Lisa and Alex worked,
was advertising for a midwife. 'You were talking
about looking for a job,' Lisa said. 'Well, you're not
fit enough yet—but the job doesn't start for a couple
of months. It'd be lovely to work in the same hospital
as you.' She winked. 'And I might need my own per-
sonalised midwife quite shortly.'

Emily reached over to hug her sister. 'Lisa, you're
not…?'

'Too early to tell properly, but I wouldn't be surprised.'

'I thought Alex was looking smug. Now I know
why.'

'He's as pleased as me, but we're not saying anything until I'm absolutely certain. Now, what d'you think of this job?'

Emily scanned the paper. 'Well, I've got everything it asks for. My recent experience is probably a lot broader than most midwives'. I've had to do things that strictly ought to be done by doctors.'

'Don't emphasise that. Some doctors are a bit jealous of what they think are their rights.'

'I know that. I think I'll apply. I'd like to work in a big hospital again, surrounded by experts and lots of equipment.'

As Lisa had been talking, Emily had been thinking of her last few days in the mission hospital, so many miles away. To be exact, she'd been thinking of Dr Stephen James. She found herself thinking of him quite frequently—and hoping that he didn't feel too badly about her. She'd never mentioned him to any of her family. She knew, of course, that he'd never bother to get in touch with her. Why should he?

The interview was testing, but she'd always been careful to keep up with the latest developments in midwifery technique and felt she acquitted herself quite well. One question was difficult. How did she feel about moving into a state-of-the-art hospital from a tiny bush hospital?

'There's going to be quite a culture shock,' she admitted frankly, 'but mums and babies are the same all over the world. I don't think I'll have any problems. And if I do I'll ask.'

It must have been the right answer. That, and the fact that Blazes had received a glowing reference from Sister O'Reilly. She was offered the job.

It wasn't to start for six weeks, and before she took

up her post she was invited to go and stay in a branch
of the mission on the south coast. The Sister in charge
wrote to say that she'd heard about Emily from Sister
O'Reilly. Emily would spend most of her time recu-
perating, but she'd also get the chance to catch up on
the latest midwifery techniques. And, in return, would
she mind talking to other volunteers who were going
out for a two-year stay, or at least thinking about it?

'A chat with someone young who's actually done
the job would be invaluable,' the Sister wrote. 'I do
hope you can help us.' Emily decided she could.

Before she took the train south two letters arrived.
One, addressed to the entire family, was from her father. He had been kidnapped by guerillas in Peru, but
had got to like them and had said he didn't want to
be rescued. In fact, when they'd offered to free him,
he'd said he'd stay and help with their little school.

'I'm very happy here,' he wrote. 'The only thing I
miss is my three girls. But now is the time that you
must spread your wings, start your own lives. I'll
come back when I'm needed for grandfathering
duties. That I am looking forward to. Until then, I
love you all.'

There was a definite lump in Emily's throat when
she read the letter. Lisa was affected, too, and even
the remote Rosalind looked a little unhappy. Life
without their ever-supportive father had been different. It had certainly made them all more self-reliant—
but they missed him.

The other letter came from Sister O'Reilly. The replacement for Emily was turning out to be a good,
useful girl. Serwalo and baby Moses had responded

well to treatment, and Sister confidently expected her to be pregnant again soon.

Had Emily seen anything of Dr James? He couldn't have had too harsh an opinion of them. Apparently, he'd spoken very highly of the mission and the government had sent extra money and equipment for them. 'This only means,' Sister wrote laconically, 'that we work harder than ever.'

Emily sighed. Her experiences in Africa now seemed almost a dream. In retrospect, it had been the right time to come home. She had been working too hard.

The gentle air on the south coast did her good. Sister McKinnon was a double of Sister O'Reilly. 'You will take things *easy*,' she said, with the air of one who expected to be obeyed. So Emily followed a programme of graduated exercise, worked out by the physiotherapist, ate well, swam a little and slept quite a lot.

As requested, she talked to the volunteers about the conditions they might expect to find. She was rather alarmed when, after listening to her, one of the volunteers decided that this kind of work was not for her and left the programme.

Sister McKinnon took a different point of view. 'You've saved us time and money, Emily. That girl would have been back inside a month. It's good for her to find out now that she's not suitable. Nothing *I* could say would put her off.'

On occasion Emily helped in the labour suite. It enabled her to become familiar with modern techniques, which really hadn't changed at all. At first Sister McKinnon wouldn't let her do too much, but eventually Emily tired of being treated as if she were an invalid.

'Look,' she said, with some exasperation, 'there's nothing wrong with me. I am fit, well and willing. My help is needed here so let me give it!'

Then she looked up and blushed to see Sister smiling at her. 'I think you're well again,' Sister said.

She took the train back north, feeling totally different from the way she'd felt coming down. She felt more confident and was looking forward to her new job and perhaps a new life. She remembered what her father had said—she needed to spread her wings. Well, she would.

For the first part of her journey the train was largely empty. But it filled after a while, and the seat opposite her was taken by a young man. She was reading the *Nursing Times*, but from behind it she was aware that the man was stealing the odd glance at her. Once she would have frozen him with a glare or even changed her seat. But she didn't.

She knew he'd speak to her, and in time he did. 'Excuse me, are you a nurse? I'm in the same trade myself. Well, I'm a medical student, actually.'

Once she would have rebuffed him. But he was a pleasant young man and she replied. They talked for the next two hours until he had to get off the train. 'Been lovely talking to you, Emily. If I come up to your wicked city, perhaps we'll meet again.'

'That would be nice. Bye, Peter.'

Only after he'd gone did she realise what she'd done. She'd had a harmless, enjoyable conversation with quite an attractive man. She knew he rather fancied her, and would perhaps have liked to see more of her. She didn't want to—he was too young, for a start—but she could deal with him. She had enjoyed his company. At long last she was coming into her own.

Her sisters could see the change in her, too. That night she had dinner at Lisa's house and everyone commented on how well she looked. 'You've put on a bit of weight,' Rosalind said. 'Mind you, you needed to. You looked like a collection of wire coat-hangers.'

'Well, thanks. Tell me, have you taken your bed-side manner exam yet?'

'Exams I pass,' Rosalind said cheerfully. 'It's just the patients that get in my way. What d'you think about Lisa's news?'

Lisa was now officially pregnant. 'I think it's tre-mendous,' Emily said. 'All those years, with her being the bossy older sister. I'm a midwife so I'm going to get my own back.'

It was good to be with her family again.

Before she was married Lisa had had a flat, which Emily was now going to take over. The day before she started work Alex gave her a hand with her trunks and boxes. She moved in, unpacking things that had been stored for over two years. There were books, pictures, ornaments. Her rooms would be for living in, nothing like the bedroom in Africa which she had deliberately kept plain. Now her new life was really starting.

Emily's new uniform was dark blue and smart. On one shoulder was the silver midwifery badge and on the other her nursing badge. It was a big change from the T-shirt and shorts she'd worn so often at the mission.

She stood in the vast car park, looking at the scurrying figures, the two giant high-rise blocks and the low buildings behind stretching out apparently indefinitely. This was modern medicine. A surge of excitement pulsed through her at the prospect of her new life. After all, she was only twenty-eight. Plenty of time to start again.

Her first shift was an early. She'd already been in to introduce herself and to look round so she knew where to go and what to do. Making her way to the maternity wing, she first had to negotiate the locked doors by flashing her security pass at the screen. No one was allowed to wander around here, unsupervised and unrecognised. There had been too many cases of babies being stolen. She shivered at the very idea of such a thing.

Too excited to have a coffee first, she walked to the nurses' station and waited for hand-over. This was where she'd be allocated her day's work. Then she'd be introduced to her mum-to-be by the midwife going off watch.

The shift leader was a grade G called Denise Coles, an amiable, rather large lady in her mid-forties. She came down early so she could introduce Emily to the other midwives on the shift. Emily thought this was thoughtful, and guessed that under her friendly exterior Denise was observant and efficient.

Emily was allocated to room three and her name was marked on the board that indicated where all the midwives were working. She was taking over from

Kathy Phillips, who smiled at her and led her the pink-painted corridor to her room.

'A primigravida called Debbie Ward,' she said, as they hurried along. 'No problems whatsoever so far and contractions now about one in ten. She is seven centimetres dilated, cervix fully effaced and central, head at minus two above the ischial spines. She came in with spontaneous rupture of the membranes and dilating regularly early this morning. At a guess, she'll go quite quickly. She's nervous but not terrified. Look out for the husband. Thank goodness he hasn't got a camcorder.'

'Camcorder?' mumbled Emily. She'd heard of husbands videoing births, but had never had to deal with the situation. She knew that giving birth was often an intensely spiritual occasion for both wife and husband, but it was also an intensely physical one, too.

Kathy giggled. 'I always have a comb handy. If hundreds of people are going to watch you in years to come, you want to look your best.'

'I'll remember to bring my lipstick in future,' Emily said dryly.

She was enjoying herself. It struck her that, without realising it, this was something she had missed. The careless camaraderie of a large ward and the sense of being one of a team were both valuable parts of a midwife's life.

It was hard to tell who was most worried, Debbie Ward or her husband, Arthur. He looked ludicrously young. His moustache only made him seem more youthful. Debbie was sitting at the head of the bed, Arthur's arm round her protectively.

'I'm off now,' Kathy said cheerfully, 'but Emily

here is taking over. Now, Debbie, I'll be in to see you tomorrow, and I want to see that cot filled.'

'Not half as much as I do,' Debbie managed to croak, and Emily hid a smile. There'd be no difficulties with this mum.

Kathy took Emily to one side and ran through the observations over the past five hours since Debbie had been admitted. Last Hb—haemoglobin—was 11.5 two months ago. Blood pressure, temperature and pulse had been fine. She had been given an antacid to prevent Mendelson's syndrome—inhalation of stomach contents—should she need to go to Theatre. So far she had been using gas and air for pain relief. Emily signed on the partogram—the record of labour. Debbie was now her responsibility.

After two hours Debbie was contracting one in five and was fully dilated and pushing well when Denise Coles came in. 'Just seeing how you were getting on,' she explained to Emily. 'Hi, Debbie, it's not going to be long now.'

Emily knew that Denise would keep an eye on her for the first week or two until she was entirely satisfied with Emily's skills. She didn't mind—she liked being part of a team that was careful.

Half an hour later Emily buzzed for a second midwife to take the baby. It was a normal delivery and the baby was a little girl. Emily gave her to the husband to hold for a moment, before putting her to her mother's breast. There were tears in Arthur's eyes. Emily thought that there was no difference between fathers in the African bush and those in the heart of European cities.

When she eventually managed to glance at her

watch some time later Emily wasn't entirely surprised to discover that four hours of her shift had passed. Being a midwife was often like that—the work carried you along with it. Still, she'd been on her feet for long enough. Things were quiet at the moment, the health care assistant was coping and Debbie, husband and baby were quite content.

'I'm going for a break now,' Emily said. 'Back in half an hour.' If anything went wrong—which was most unlikely—anyone could press the buzzer.

Outside in the corridor she leaned backwards, pushed her arms over her head. After bending over for so long it was always a good idea to stretch. Then she set off towards the nurses' office, where there was always coffee available.

A doctor came out of one of the little rooms and walked down the corridor ahead of her. She knew he was a doctor by the long white coat and the stethoscope, looped round his neck. He was limping badly, but his body looked athletic.

Casually she noted the dark hair, the powerful line of his shoulders, the trim waist. Even though he was limping he was moving quickly—like someone she knew. Her eyes fastened on him as a passing fancy turned into wild suspicion and then an appalled certainty. He was the last man on earth she expected to see here. The word was torn from her before she could stop it. 'Stephen!' she cried.

He stopped and turned slowly, as if not wanting to. His face was white, with an expression of disbelief. As he saw her and grasped fully who she was, the colour came back to his cheeks—and with it an expression of ferocious anger.

'Not you! What are you doing here?' The question was ground out, as if just seeing her caused him pain.

Bewildered, she said, 'I've just started today. I'm the new midwife.'

'You are? Why wasn't I told?' He seemed to think there was some kind of conspiracy to keep him in the dark.

'There was no secret about it,' she said defensively. 'The job was advertised and I applied.'

'Of all the hospitals in the country, you had to pick this one. Why?'

She supposed he was entitled to be angry at her still, but there was a limit to what she would take. 'You sound like Rick out of *Casablanca*,' she said. 'Are you trying to be a new Humphrey Bogart?'

If possible, his face got angrier than ever. 'I should have remembered that you always had something to say for yourself,' he snarled, 'even when it wasn't particularly useful or clever. Now, listen. I didn't know you were being appointed here—if I had known I would have objected very strongly. But you are here. I'm Specialist Registrar in this department.

'Get one thing straight. This is not the African bush. Here you do your job and no one else's. Don't make decisions for other people. If I catch you making one mistake, doing one job that isn't yours, I'll have you sacked.'

By now she, too, was angry. 'You won't need to. If I make one mistake I'll resign. But don't think I've changed. If I had to, I'd make the same decision again. Surely missing one game of rugby wasn't that bad?'

The bitterest of smiles spread across his face. 'I

.ven't played rugby since I last saw you. And I
on't again.'

Meeting Stephen so unexpectedly had quite thrown
Emily. Often she'd wondered to herself if they would
ever meet again and if so whether he would have mellowed towards her. She had very much hoped that he
would. But he seemed angrier than ever. This was
quite upsetting her first day. Why was he overreacting
so? She had thought better of him.

'Look,' she said, 'it seems that we have to work
together. I didn't know you were here but, since you
are, we'll have to make the best of it.'

'The best of it,' he echoed. 'Just make sure you
don't get in my way, midwife. And be very, very sure
that you don't take any more of my decisions.' He
turned and strode down the corridor.

Shaken, Emily went to the nurses' room. She didn't
want coffee now, but she had to write up her notes.
Meeting Stephen like this had quite ruined her day.
And underneath was the niggling suspicion that she
had hoped, against all the evidence, that if they ever
did meet again he would have forgiven her. She was
surprised to realise how badly she wanted Stephen's
good opinion.

Apparently casually, the next day she mentioned to
Denise Coles that she'd run into the specialist registrar. She didn't say that she'd met him before.

'Young Stephen,' said the smiling Denise. 'He's a
good doctor, that one. Walks down the corridor as if
he's in a race—quite puffs me to keep up. But he
pushes himself hardest, and he recognises good work.
You'll enjoy working with him, Emily.'

'I'm sure I will,' Emily said.

Apart from that, the rest of the week was enjoy_
Debbie Ward left with her precious baby, Gail, pr_
ing a box of chocolates on all the staff before s_
went. There was a postpartum haemorrhage _
Emily's third day, and she was quite shocked to dis_
cover that she had to send for a senior house officer,
instead of dealing with it herself. The young doctor
was nervous and anxious, and his feelings affected his
patient. I could have done that better, she thought
afterwards, then caught herself. She wasn't a doctor.

She didn't see Stephen again for the rest of her first
week, but she found herself looking for him and wondered why.

Emily was quite tired by the end of the week, and
very happy to accept Lisa's invitation to come round
for a family dinner. She now felt that she was part of
the family, Alex, Jack, Holly and Lucy all made her
feel welcome. Rosalind was there, of course, and a
couple of family friends—Harry Shea and his wife,
Sally.

At first Emily found Harry a bit frightening—he
was a massive man with a bald head, who played an
evil drug dealer in a television soap which was made
at the other side of the city. But after she'd talked to
him for a while she found he was sweet—not at all
like the character he played.

'You might be able to help me, Emily,' he said, as
they sat drinking coffee after dinner. 'A friend of
mine called Ben Crosby will be nosing round your
wards over the next few weeks. He's going to play a
young gynaecologist on the series, and he's got permission to poke around to try to get a bit of back-

ground knowledge. He looks very confident but, in fact, he's quite shy. Like me, he has to act.'

'I'll look out for him,' Emily promised. 'Apart from you, I've never met an actor before.'

Harry and his wife had to leave early. Apparently Harry's hours were long and he started early. Lucy said she'd put the children to bed so Emily was left with her two sisters and new brother-in-law, happily chatting around the fire.

'So, how's your first week been?' Alex asked lazily. 'Bit of a culture shock after Africa?'

'You could say that. But I'm enjoying it. It's not any easier, though—the work's just as tough.'

'No problems, settling in?'

'No-o,' she said, then wondered why her voice sounded so doubtful. At first she wasn't going to mention it but then she remembered how once before she hadn't confided in her family, hadn't let them help her. And look what had happened.

'There is something a bit, well, upsetting, I suppose,' she said. 'I met the specialist registrar in Africa, and I don't think he's got a very good opinion of me. But I still think I was right.'

She told the story of how she'd kept Stephen at the mission, not concealing the fact that she knew she'd done wrong.

'Typical piece of Emily behaviour,' Rosalind commented. 'I sympathise with you, but you can't really carry on like that, can you?'

'I think he might have calmed down a bit by now,' Lisa said.

Alex said nothing, and when Emily looked at him

he seemed troubled. She was surprised as she thought he, too, might have sympathised.

'When you caught hepatitis, Emily,' he said, 'I gather you were out of things—didn't know what was happening, took no interest in the big world.'

'That's right. Much of the time I just slept.'

'You wouldn't know, then. I didn't know about your part in the story but I'm afraid there's more to it.'

Emily felt apprehensive. Somehow she knew she wasn't going to like what was coming.

Alex didn't seem happy about telling her, either, and this increased her distress. She suspected he was trying to make things easy for her. Eventually he said, 'I know Stephen quite well. I didn't know why he missed his plane, only that he was determined to get to Johannesburg somehow. Anyway, at the airport he managed to persuade a local to fly him south in a light plane—a man called Carl Rodriguez.'

'No!' Emily was horrified. She knew Carl Rodriguez by reputation. He would do anything for money. 'The man's a crook!'

'He's dead now,' Alex said. 'The plane crashed in the bush. Apparently, it was quite unsafe. Rodriguez was killed instantly. Search parties went out when the plane didn't arrive. They found Stephen after two days. Apart from being generally banged about, he'd smashed his ankle, a compound fracture of the medial malleolus. There was a lot of ligament damage, too. He'd tried to set it himself—made himself a rough box splint.

'Then he sat there, without water, and waited. Only his native toughness enabled him to survive. The search parties got there only just in time. But he'll always limp, and he'll never play rugby again.'

Emily sat motionless. She knew better than any of them the cruelty of the bush. She knew what Stephen must have gone through. 'He blames me for what happened,' she said, 'and he's right. I'm responsible for him crashing and breaking his leg. I can't blame him for hating me.'

It was Rosalind who reached over to hug her in the old family custom. 'You didn't know,' she said. 'It's foolish to blame yourself.'

'No, it's not,' Emily said bitterly. 'Just think what you'd all think if it had been me on that plane.'

The other three thought about it. And Emily could tell that her remark had struck home. They would have wanted to blame someone. No one spoke.

'When he spoke to me last Monday he must have thought I knew about his accident. No wonder he was angry. He must have thought me completely insensitive. I'm going to have to explain things to him and tell him how really sorry I am, but I don't want to see him in hospital. D'you know his home address, Alex? I'll have to call round.'

Alex nodded. 'I've got it in my book. But are you sure it's the right thing to do? Do you want to do it?'

She shook her head miserably. 'It's the last thing I want to do.'

'Then why not keep quiet and let things ride?'

Rosalind leaned over to punch her new brother-in-law. 'You don't know our Em yet, do you? She'll do what she thinks is right—and no one will talk her out of it.'

'Look where doing what I thought was right has

got me,' Emily said. 'Lisa, I think I'd like to go home, if you don't mind. I'm not going to be good company for anyone tonight. There's something I've got to do.' She had intended to stay the night.

Lisa knew her sister. 'If that's what you want. But ring us when you've got some news.'

Emily nodded. She refused Alex's offer to run her back. She felt she needed the walk. 'I'll phone tomorrow night if there's any news,' she said. 'Love to you all.' She left, feeling guilty at spoiling what had been a very pleasant family evening.

On the way home she managed to avoid thinking by the expedient of walking so hard that her lungs burned and her legs ached. But once she was in her own tiny living room she had to face up to what she had done.

Only she knew the full cruelty of the bush, of what the heat, the insects and the lack of water could do to a wounded man. And, again, she thought she was the only person there who had actually been in a bad crash. She didn't think about it so often now but there had been a time when she'd thought of little else.

Hers had been a car crash, not a plane crash, but she thought that the experiences would be similar. There was the sick knowledge of being out of control. There was always time for realisation, even if there was no time to do anything. The powerlessness, the explosion of pain, the noise—all were imprinted on her memory. It was horrible.

And the time in hospital afterwards was, if anything, worse. There was the misery and the desperate need to blame someone else. Now she knew what Stephen James felt about her. No one better.

CHAPTER FIVE

NEXT morning Emily woke early. Perhaps it was the hangover from the week of earlies she'd just worked. Whatever it was, she just couldn't lie there and enjoy her anticipated lie-in. She was uneasy in bed and even though she was tired, she had to get up and do something.

Pulling on a pair of jeans and a sweater, she set off for the seafront. It wasn't far, and she enjoyed walking the broad beach with the sea on one side and sandhills on the other. There was a gentle breeze and the tart ammonia smell of the shore. It had to be nearly high tide as ships were in line in the channel, making for the port.

This was a different beach from the lonely, black-sanded one where she had first met Stephen. But it struck a chord in her memory, and for a while she relived the precious moments when she'd first met him. He'd aroused feelings in her that she'd thought long dead, and for that, she supposed, she owed him something. She'd thanked him in a poor way. Angrily she strode on, the sand squeaking under her boots.

She wasn't looking forward to this coming meeting. She felt guilty, and she didn't like it. She'd have to eat humble pie, and if he was still angry with her she'd have to take it. But she was conscious that a tiny part of her did want to see him. This was the man who had kissed her—whom she had kissed back. She pushed the thought aside and turned for home.

The brisk walk had brought the flush of youth to her cheeks, highlighting her eyes. But she didn't want to appear happy and healthy. He might take it as an insult. He'd been proud of his skill at rugby and had enjoyed playing. What would he think of the woman who'd stopped that enjoyment?

What should she wear that was suitably penitential? After checking her wardrobe, she decided that the clothes for being sorry in were a plain skirt and a black sweater. After showering and dressing, she realised that she was still far too early. After all, this was Saturday morning.

He might still be in bed. There was a sudden flash of the memory of waking him in the middle of the night to ask for his help. She pushed the thought aside. She knew he wasn't on duty because she'd asked Alex.

Then she realised she was putting it off. Whichever way it went, this meeting was bound to change their relationship. Such as it was. She sighed, and set off to walk to his address.

His flat was not too far from hers. A lot of hospital people lived out here. But the block was bigger, the flats obviously more expensive.

Not really thinking about it, she walked up to the front door just as a family was walking in. She didn't need to operate the entryphone. Good. She didn't want their conversation to start through a small metal grill.

His flat was on the third floor. Stiffening her resolve, she knocked on it smartly. At first there was no answer—she wondered if she'd nerved herself for an ordeal and no one was going to be in.

There was. She heard the sound of quick steps, the door started to open and she braced herself—and there was a woman.

Emily looked at her in surprise and some disappointment. She realised she had seen the woman on her ward. She was a senior house officer, Lyn Taylor, who constantly took the observations that nurses and midwifes weren't allowed to do. She was older than the average house doctor. To Emily they now all seemed to be pinkly young. But this one was older. She had tightly permed blonde hair and rather a lot of lipstick. Over smart trousers and sweater she was wearing a man's apron.

The two women looked at each other. Neither seemed pleased to see the other.

'Yes?' asked the blonde doctor coldly.

Emily supposed that there was no reason why Stephen shouldn't have female friends, especially ones on his ward. Perhaps this woman was even closer than a friend—she could be a lover. An uncharitable part of her reckoned that he could do better than this, but she suppressed the thought. However, she was disappointed.

'I'm sorry to bother you,' Emily offered eventually, 'but I thought Dr James lived here. Could I see him, please?'

It wasn't the right thing to ask. As she surveyed the trim figure in front of her, the blonde's expression grew even more frigid. 'He does live here,' she conceded, 'but at the moment he's out. Is there anything I can do? Perhaps if you give me your name?'

She didn't recognise Emily. It was obvious that, for this doctor, nurses, midwives and so on were part of the furniture, not people in their own right.

Emily said, 'My name is Emily Grey. I've just started as a midwife in Ward 17. I work with Dr James—and you, for that matter. Dr James and I met in Africa. There's something personal I have to explain to him.'

'Something personal?' the woman asked sharply.

Emily decided not to get upset or angry, but she was wishing she hadn't come. She hadn't bargained for this. 'Personal but not sexual,' she said acidly. 'I'm sorry I disturbed you. I'll phone again later. Good morning.'

The woman smiled rapidly, opened the door further and motioned for Emily to enter. 'Do come in. My name's Dr Taylor—Lyn Taylor, by the way. I'm sorry if I was a little short with you, but Stephen does get troubled at times by silly little nurses.'

'I am not a silly little nurse,' Emily said, wondering if perhaps she was.

'Of course not.' They entered a pleasant corner living room, with windows on two sides. Emily was waved to a seat. 'I've just popped round to help Stephen with his housework. It's the least you can do for your fiancé.'

'Is he your fiancé?' Emily queried, startled. She looked at Lyn's ringless hand.

Dr Taylor saw the glance. 'He certainly is. We've know each other for a long time, but medical work being what it is we've never got round to formalising things.'

'I see.' Emily felt disappointed, and more than ever

convinced she'd made a mistake in coming here. Stephen had kissed her when he'd had a fiancée at home. Perhaps it had only been a kiss—but it could have grown into something a lot more.

Lyn had now obviously decided to be friends. 'I'll fetch us both a coffee, shall I? Then perhaps I can help you.'

Emily looked around the room when she'd left. It was friendly, slightly cluttered, the room of a man who had a variety of interests. There were books on all sorts of subjects, a pile of CDs, medical prints arranged on one wall. She leaned forward and peered through a telescope at a ship, moving slowly up the estuary. She'd like to spend more time in a room like this.

Lyn returned with the coffee. 'Can you give me some hint of what your problem is? Perhaps I can help? Stephen has been under an awful lot of pressure recently, with his new job and that dreadful accident in Africa. I've had a terrible time with him.'

She seemed genuinely solicitous, and the reference to the accident convinced Emily. She was already regretting having come here. She'd tell her story and let this woman approach Stephen.

'Well,' she said hesitantly, 'I'm sure he'll tell you. In fact, I suppose I'm the one responsible for the accident...'

Lyn was a good listener. She didn't interrupt as Emily poured out her story, and didn't indicate in any way that she found Emily to blame. Emily explained why she wanted to apologise again to Stephen because she hadn't known about his accident.

When she did speak, Lyn seemed to sympathise

with Emily. 'Stephen's always been an awkward man,' she said. 'Once he's decided on something nothing can change his mind. And I do 'think you were right about the rugby match. He should have stayed behind with your patient. But he hates being crossed. I'm afraid you've made an enemy.'

'Just what I wanted to hear,' muttered Emily.

Lyn sipped her coffee, apparently thinking. Eventually she said, 'You know, I don't think Stephen will want to hear about this. He's been through hell, and he'll only think you're trying to settle your own conscience. I know he won't want another apology. Take my word, it'll only anger and upset him. You don't really want to apologise, do you?'

'I feel I ought to,' Emily said honestly, 'but it isn't something I want to do.'

'Then don't say anything. I'll probe a bit, and if I think it'll do any good I'll tell you. Is that all right? We both want the same thing, don't we? We want him to be happy.'

'If you say so.' Emily felt uneasy. This conversation hadn't gone the way she'd expected. She wanted to talk to Stephen, not the woman who claimed to be his fiancée. And now Lyn was picking up her cup in a way which indicated that the interview was over. 'I guess I'll be off, then,' Emily said, and stood.

'Now, don't forget what we've agreed,' Lyn said, showing her to the door. 'See you around on the ward.'

'On the ward,' Emily agreed, and walked downstairs.

As she walked home she felt dissatisfied. She had an uneasy feeling that she'd been outmanoeuvred. All right, Lyn was his fiancée, but she seemed to be taking too many decisions for the man she was going to marry. And as she thought that, Emily grew more uneasy than ever. She thought she'd got to know Stephen, even though they'd only been together for a few days. And she couldn't see him marrying someone like Lyn. But the woman was obviously at home in his flat... Emily shook her head in frustration. If she'd been Stephen, she would have wanted an explanation. It was odd.

She was happy to be back at work. Her workmates were a friendly lot and she was getting to know them, hearing about their families and their boyfriends. It was a good, tight-knit unit. Denise Coles had now decided that Emily was quite competent and didn't wander in and out any more.

'I've put you in charge of Annette Spring,' Denise said at change-over two days later. She's a primigravida and had a long first stage. Now at four centimetres but not contracting very well. Trouble is, she's anxious. You'll need to calm her.'

'I can cope,' Emily said cheerfully.

'I know you can. Dr James will be in to review her at about eleven. She's had a few decelerations and isn't progressing well.'

Dr James? Emily wondered if she could cope.

Looking after Annette was difficult. Either she complained or she cried. Emily tried to cheer her up, asking her about plans for the future and talking about baby's names—the usual topics that kept mothers-to-be happy. None of them worked.

Promptly at eleven Stephen arrived. The first she

knew was when the door opened and he walked past her with a crisp nod.

'Morning Mrs Spring—it's Annette, isn't it? I'm Dr James and I'm yet another person who's come to ask you a great list of irritating questions.' He offered his hand to be shaken.

Emily had had nothing but complaints from Annette all morning, but Stephen got a smile. What a bedside manner, Emily thought, irritated. But she'd seen it before. Somehow, if a patient could be charmed then Stephen would charm her.

He looked well. Under his medical coat a pure white shirt, tucked into dark trousers, emphasised the trim waist. He wore a blue and silver silk tie from some college that she didn't recognise. His face was animated, his eyes sparkled and those devastating lips made her think of...

Then he turned to her, and it was as if a storm cloud had eclipsed the sun. His face was a cold mask. 'The notes, please?' Even his voice was curt.

That decided her. He was entirely entitled to dislike her but he'd listen to her first. She wasn't going to wait for Lyn to negotiate some kind of half-settlement.

Dealing with Annette didn't take long. Stephen said to her, 'Well, Annette, you're doing fine but I think we need to hurry you up a bit. We need your contractions to be a bit stronger and a bit more frequent then we can get this baby out quicker. With your permission, I'm going to give you a drip which contains syntocinon. That should do the trick.'

'Whatever you say, Doctor,' Annette whispered.

He turned to Emily. 'Are you qualified to insert a

Venflon?' A venflon was a fixed needle into the vein in the back of the hand, a means of introducing a drip into the system.

'Certainly,' Emily said.

'And you've used syntocinon before?'

'Very often.'

'I'll leave you to it, then.' He turned to go. And as he turned to leave Emily caught him at the door. 'Dr James, do you think you could give me five minutes of your time?'

He frowned at her. 'Is there something you've not told me?' he asked quietly, indicating Annette.

She shook her head. 'No. This is an entirely personal matter.'

'Personal? Between us?' he asked, as if the very idea was ridiculous.

She flushed. 'I'm afraid so. It won't take long.'

'Is it important?'

'I think it is. Perhaps you will, too.'

'Very well, then, if it's just five minutes. The sitting room appeared to be vacant just now.'

They walked to the room where visitors sometimes waited. It was full of dog-eared magazines, with a glass wall into the corridor. He didn't sit down. 'Well?'

She hadn't had time to prepare a speech as she'd only just decided to approach him. For a second she searched for words and then, in a rush, she said, 'I'm sorry to go over old ground, and I know your fiancée said that you wouldn't like this, but I've got to say it.'

She noted his look of surprise, but now she'd started she had to hurry on. 'I only found out about your accident last week—breaking your leg, that is. When you left the mission I was…very ill. I'd contracted hepatitis A. I had to be invalided out to Golanda and then to Johannesburg. I wasn't conscious of what was happening in the world around me for a couple of months. And people must have kept the news of your accident from me deliberately.'

'Are you suggesting that you were ill when you stopped me leaving the mission?'

'No,' she said quickly. 'That was a conscious decision I took, and I take full responsibility for it. I knew what I was doing. I've regretted it a dozen times since, but that's no consolation to you. I just never guessed that you'd…well, that you'd break your leg. And you can't ever play rugby again. I didn't know about your accident last week so what I said then must have seemed very self-righteous.

'I just want to say I'm even more sorry than I was before. If that's possible. And the reason I didn't get in touch in Africa was that I didn't know. I just wish I'd been told.'

Perhaps his face was slightly less forbidding than it had been. Neutrally he said, 'Well, if you've learned not to take other people's decisions for them then that's a good thing.' He rubbed his lower lip with his finger, a gesture she remembered. 'You say you spoke to my fiancée?'

'Yes—Dr Taylor. When I called round at your flat last Saturday morning. She said that telling you would be the wrong thing to do, but I just couldn't say nothing. I hope you're not too upset?' She looked at him anxiously.

He frowned, but she had the impression that she

wasn't the cause of it. 'I can probably cope,' he said. 'After all, I've had practice.'

'I'm even more in your debt than I realised,' she went on miserably. 'I want you to know that if there's anything I can do to wipe out part of the debt, I will.'

'Anything?' he asked sardonically, and this time she felt herself blushing.

'You know what I mean. And thank you for listening to me.'

'Yes. Just don't take any more of my decisions, will you?'

'Never,' she said fervently. 'Never.'

He turned to go. His back had been to the glass wall, and just before he turned Emily caught a flash of white coat in the corridor outside. It was Lyn. And her expression was vengeful.

Emily walked slowly back to her room. She wasn't quite sure how her explanation and apology had been taken, but she was glad she'd given them.

She turned a corner and there outside her room was Lyn—white-faced with anger. Grabbing Emily by the arm, she snarled, 'I want a word with you! What have you been saying to Dr James?'

Emily was surprised at the force of the grip. She looked down silently until her arm was released then she said coolly, 'I was telling him that I hadn't known it was my fault he'd broken his leg, and I was sorry for it.'

'I told you not to speak to him!' The words were spat out.

'I'm afraid that was a decision that only I could make. I felt had to speak to him.'

The doctor now seemed almost beside herself with

rage. 'You won't leave him alone. You're like all the rest of the nurses around here. I suppose you threw yourself at him in Africa!'

She hadn't, but the memory of the kiss on the beach came back to haunt her and her heightened colour betrayed her.

'I might have guessed so! Leave him alone! He's going to marry me!'

Lyn turned and strode down the corridor. Emily sighed. It was bad enough to work with Stephen but at least he was only in the ward on occasion. The house officers were in and out all the time. She was going to see a lot of Dr Taylor and she knew she'd have to do everything exactly right. Life was going to be complicated.

She fixed up the IV line to Annette's arm and went to the fridge for the syntocinon. After asking the nearest midwife to check with her the name, the amount and the date, she went back to Annette and injected the syntocinon into the bag of Hartman's solution. Then she started the drip via an acuset and an IMED, and keyed in the initial dose of six millilitres per hour on the little keypad. Then she went to the CTG machine. From now on she would monitor the foetal heart rate continuously.

Over the next two hours she gradually increased the drip rate to the maximum of ninety-six millilitres per hour. Then she noticed the baby's heart rate had dropped dramatically. It didn't quickly return to the baseline so she turned down the syntocinon dose to forty-eight millilitres per hour. The heart beat picked up.

She checked her fob watch. It was time for hand-over. Annette still showed little signs of progress when she said goodbye. She walked over to the nurses' station, carefully avoiding looking at Lyn Taylor who was in the corridor. Instead she greeted Rachel Roberts, a young friendly midwife, recently married. 'I'm taking over from you in Room 21,' Rachel said cheerfully. 'What have you to tell me?'

'Young girl, quite anxious, got a syntocinon drip for failure to progress. Baby had a big deceleration at maximum dose so I decreased it. Otherwise everything is fine.'

'Lead me to her,' said Rachel.

The next day was a nightmare.

Unusually for her, Denise Coles wasn't smiling. 'Could you come into my office please, Miss Grey?' Her approach was definitely unfriendly, not only the use of her surname but Denise's entire manner. Emily wondered what was wrong. She was soon to find out.

'Yesterday you gave syntocinon to Annette Spring,' Denise said, when they were alone.

'Yes I did. She was up to the maximum dose of ninety-six millilitres. The baby's heart rate dropped so I lowered it to forty-eight millilitres.'

'Yes, that's marked on the partogram. Now tell me why Mrs Spring was still getting ninety-six millilitres when Rachel Roberts took over.'

Emily stared at Denise blankly. 'She wasn't! She couldn't have, I lowered it.'

'No, you didn't. Fortunately, Rachel Roberts *is* conscientious. She checked everything and found the dosage too high. Very properly, she called me. The mother and child were in no danger, of course, but I don't like to think of what might have happened if you'd left the dosage high in the middle of your shift.'

'Neither was harmed?' Emily's horror was evident and Denise's features relaxed slightly at Emily's concern.

'But you still made a mistake. It's not hard to mark something on the partogram, and then think you've already done it. Either you left the syntocinon at ninety-six or you raised it again. You could have put the baby in danger.'

'But...' There was nothing Emily could say. Mistakes were made in medicine—but she was sure she hadn't made this one.

'Dr James wasn't at all impressed,' Denise went on grimly. 'He came in while Rachel Roberts was reporting to me. I told him this was a matter for me to deal with, not him. It's a nursing matter, not a medical one. But if I were you I'd try to stay away from him for a while.'

Stephen! What would he think of her?

'What do I do now?' Emily asked.

'They're short-staffed on the postnatal ward. You can go and lend a hand on the low-dependency unit.'

'But I'm—'

'Off you go. They're expecting you.' There was nothing more she could say. Emily went to the low-dependency unit.

This was a punishment. She was being given unimportant work to do because she couldn't be trusted. The low-dependency unit was only half-full, and things were made worse when she heard that a midwife was being sent to the delivery suite. She had been replaced.

Miserably, she went about the menial tasks that were given to her. She was worth better than this. Or was she?

Lunchtime came. Desolately she went to sit in the far corner of the canteen and ate her bowl of salad hidden behind a pillar. She didn't want people, didn't want to talk. Constantly she revolved yesterday's happenings in her mind. She was *sure* she'd lowered the dosage. How had it got up again?

She saw Stephen come in. Like her, he chose a bowl of salad and took it to a distant table. She shrank back behind her pillar, knowing he wouldn't come to sit with her but not wanting him even to see her. What must he think of her? He might dislike her for what she'd done to him in Africa, but at least he knew she was a competent nurse and midwife. For Stephen to doubt her professional skill was almost the worst part of what had happened. She remembered she'd told him she'd resign if she made a mistake. Perhaps she should.

As she watched his table she saw Lyn walk by, holding her tray. She appeared to be surprised to see Stephen, and smiled animatedly and went to sit with him. If you think she just turned up by chance, you're a fool, Emily thought.

She couldn't bear to watch the two, with their heads together, talking and smiling. Once again she mentally went over yesterday's terrible events.

Suddenly, realisation hit her. She stood, made her way carefully to the ladies' toilet, leaned over a basin and was violently sick. It couldn't be true. But she was certain it was.

CHAPTER SIX

FORTUNATELY, no one had seen her. Emily washed her face, combed her hair and decided to abandon the rest of her salad. Then, slowly and unsteadily, she walked back to her ward.

By the time she got there she was more in control of herself. The nausea was still inside her, but she could feel anger there, too. Some of her new friends were sitting in the nurses' room, and as she helped herself to a cup of coffee she asked a couple of casual questions. The answers nearly made her sick again—but she said nothing.

That afternoon she carried on with her menial work, wondering what to do. Fury built up in her. She would not put up with this! Then the decision was made for her. She saw Stephen walking rapidly down the corridor and ran after him.

He must have heard the sound of her feet and he turned, surprised. When he saw who it was his face took on an icy expression, if anything even more forbidding than yesterday's. 'Miss Grey?'

The glacial tone would have unnerved her yesterday, but she wasn't worried now. She was angry. 'I'm afraid I have to have another private word with you, Dr James. I'm sorry to take up your time again.' She knew she didn't sound very sorry.

'I think I've already heard as much as I want from you. Now, I'm very busy and—'

'You're going to hear some more. Shall we go in the waiting room again or shall we scream in the corridor?'

For a moment she thought she'd gone too far. The sheer venom in his expression appalled her, but she stood her ground.

'This had better be important,' he said through gritted teeth, and led her her to the fortunately empty room. 'Now, if this is about yesterday's fiasco, I don't want an apology. For a start, it should go to Mrs Spring, not to me.'

'We'll talk about an apology in a minute,' she said. 'And you might change your mind.'

Now she'd got him alone, she wasn't sure where to start. There were so many things, burning to be said. Unevenly, she started. 'Dr James, you've seen me work. Weren't you surprised that I'd apparently made a stupid mistake like that?'

He paused, before answering. 'Yes, I was surprised. We have had our differences, but I'd always thought you competent. It just shows how wrong my judgement can be.'

That did it. 'Your judgement wasn't wrong. Yesterday I said that I was in your debt, and that if there was anything I could do for you I would. Well, I'm doing it now. I'll take the blame for overdosing Mrs Spring. But just you tell your fiancée, Dr Taylor, that that's the last time she interferes with one of the patients in my care.'

He stared at her and then laughed incredulously. 'This isn't worthy of you, Miss Grey. Don't try to evade responsibility. You made a mistake, and you can't blame Dr Taylor. She has had nothing to do with Mrs Spring.'

'Strange, then, that she walked into my room the minute I walked out. You're right, there was no good reason for her to be there.'

In his eyes she saw the first flicker of doubt, quickly extinguished. 'If she did, I'm sure she had good reason,' he said. 'SHOs are constantly in and out of patients' rooms. And she's been a nurse herself, you know. She wouldn't make such a gross error.'

'But I would? You're missing the point, Dr James. She altered the dosage on purpose.'

Now he, too, was angry. 'That's the most ludicrous thing I ever heard. You're raving! Why would she do that? It would be deliberately harming a patient.'

'She didn't harm a patient, she harmed me—or my professional reputation. She did it because she's desperately in love with you and sees me as a challenge. Which, incidentally, I'm not. So she tried to have me blamed for incompetence.'

Emily was really angry now. In the corridor outside she saw curious faces turn in their direction. People obviously guessed they were having some kind of row. She didn't care.

'You're mad! No doctor, no nurse, could ever do anything like that.' The sheer enormity of what Emily was suggesting seemed to drive the anger out of him. 'And she is not my fiancée. We're just friends, that's all.'

'She doesn't think that. I'll bet she sees you every chance she has. She'll be around, whether you want her or not. Has she any other boyfriends? Stop getting angry and think logically, Dr James.'

After the raised voices, the angry tones, there was an odd moment of silence. It seemed as if the anger drained from both of them. Emily felt exhausted and close to tears, which was unusual for her. He was white-faced again. He turned awkwardly and put weight on his damaged leg, and she saw him wince. 'I'm sorry if your leg hurts,' she said quietly.

His voice was low, controlled now as he replied. 'I'm sure you're wrong about Dr Taylor. But I will take you seriously and I'll look into it. Until then we'll say nothing more about it.'

He reached for the doorhandle. Before he went she thought she could again see the doubt in his eyes. But then he said, 'On the other hand, if I find that you are deliberately trying to blame your mistakes on an innocent person, I shall suggest very strongly that you resign at once.'

Emily decided to have an early night, it had been a hard, traumatic day. First she wrote a few letters and gave the flat a quick, unnecessary clean. Then she had a luxurious bath and put on the long T-shirt with Mickey Mouse on the front that she used as a nightie.

She settled down to watch TV. Harry Shea was playing Mick Mort, and she was amazed again at how such a gentle, witty man could turn into an evil, snarling drug dealer. There had been no television at the mission, and since she'd come back she'd turned into a bit of an addict.

Her doorbell rang. At this hour of the night it was certain to be Rosalind—she often dropped in—so she opened the door. And there was Stephen.

They stared at each other. He was dressed casually

in trousers and an open-necked, short-sleeved shirt. And she was in her nightie. Some kind of unspoken communication passed between them as he looked at her. She knew he was aware of the soft curve of her breasts and her bare legs. And she didn't mind.

'Sorry,' he apologised eventually. 'I didn't realise it was so late. I'd better go.'

She didn't hesitate. 'No, I was thinking of having an early night, but I certainly wasn't going to bed just yet. D'you want to come in?'

Now he hesitated. 'I wanted to speak with you,' he said, 'and not anywhere on the ward or even in the hospital. But I don't want to—'

'You won't be intruding,' she interrupted. 'D'you want tea or coffee?'

'Tea would be nice,' he said, and stepped inside.

She took him to her living room and went to put on a dressing-gown and check if she had any biscuits. When she'd made tea they sat at each side of the coffee-table and looked at each other.

She couldn't help remembering the last time they'd been really alone. There had been only one occasion—by the pool in the mountains. At the mission there had always been someone nearby, and the hospital, too, was busy. But here they were, alone together again, and she felt more than the faintest thrill of excitement.

Stephen was ill at ease. He took a biscuit and broke it into halves, then quarters. He tasted his tea and looked around, as if seeking inspiration from the furniture. 'This is a handy little flat,' he said, 'just right for one person.'

'It was my sister's. She's just got married to Alex Scott. I believe you know him.'

He looked at her, surprised. 'I didn't know Alex was your brother-in-law.'

'My sister works in infectious diseases with him.'

'I know her! I should have guessed—that gorgeous red hair you both have.'

She liked the reference to gorgeous red hair. 'I applied for this job, without telling anyone about my relations,' she said anxiously.

He nodded. 'I might have guessed that. Sometimes having relations in high places can be…delicate.'

'You're thinking about your father?'

'I am. Though it's very handy if I have problems. I just ring him up.'

The sudden burst of conversation lapsed. Eventually she said, 'I know this isn't a social visit. You have every right to dislike me. So it must be about Dr Taylor. What have you found out?'

He laughed, but with no great mirth. 'I knew you wouldn't avoid a fight, Miss Grey. It's one of your more…endearing characteristics. Yes, I talked to Dr Taylor. She denied your accusations—most vehemently, I might add. She also said I should be careful, that you were throwing yourself at me.'

Emily felt a sickening sense of disappointment. Couldn't he see what Lyn was like? He must be far more insensitive than she'd thought. 'So that's that,' she muttered.

He seemed to have regained his confidence. He sipped his tea, before saying, 'No, that isn't that. I didn't believe her. I'd made a couple of enquiries myself. I spoke to Mrs Spring, and then I spoke to Lyn

again. It took a while but I forced the truth out of her.
She said you were only making up to me, and that
you'd be better out of nursing.' His face took on a
bleak look. 'I told her to leave the ward at once. I
thought of making an official complaint to the G.M.C.
She could be thrown out of medicine altogether.'

Emily was shocked. This was a side of Stephen
she'd never seen. She'd seen the dedicated professional and the charming man who could be such good
company. Now she was seeing a ruthless, steel-hard
man, who did what he thought was right no matter
what the consequences. She reminded herself that this
was the injured man who'd kept himself alive for two
days in the bush—largely by sheer will-power.

But she had her own point of view. 'I said I'd take
the blame for her,' she said. 'That wasn't an idle offer.
I owe you that.'

He smiled thinly. 'I appreciate the offer. But you're
only a small part of the situation. What Lyn did to
you was wrong, but what she could have done to a
patient—and a pregnant one at that—was unforgivable. She's meant to be a doctor, and in this country
that is an honourable calling. She let us all down. I'd
be as bad as her if I let her get away with anything
like this. The one thing in her favour was that she
made quite sure that the patient came to no harm. She
watched and saw the relief midwife correct the dosage
at once. She had that much probity.'

Emily looked at him directly. 'So, tell me why she
did it.'

He looked uncomfortable. 'She felt she had a claim
on me. She was sure we would get married in time.

When I came to my senses, she said. She knew I loved her if I could only see it.'

'Had she any reason for thinking that?' Emily pressed.

He shrugged. 'If you mean, did we have an affair— no. I helped her and looked on her as a friend. I'm afraid she came to look on me as something more.'

'It doesn't say much for your powers of observation, Doctor, does it?'

He winced. 'Emily, I've seen you nurse. I thought you were kind, compassionate. Aren't I entitled to a bit of your sympathy?'

He'd called her Emily. She was glad, but... 'I agree with you that any doctor who knowingly harms a patient is evil, but think of her as sick, not wicked. Don't some of our mums-to-be act in odd ways? Because of their hormones? We don't blame them for it.'

He looked at her oddly. 'You're defending her, Emily. After what she did to you.'

Emily shook her head. 'I'm not defending her. I hate the woman. But she can be treated.'

'So what would you do with her?'

'I'd make sure she gets counselling. I think she's been more stupid than evil.'

He rubbed his lip with his finger. Why should such an action excite her so much? He said, 'I'll think about that, but I'll make my own mind up.'

'Good,' she said. 'I wouldn't want to make another of your decisions, would I?' Then she stopped, appalled at what she had just said.

He looked at her, shaking his head in disbelief. 'Emily,' he said, 'you are incredible.'

She decided this was a compliment, but it made her

uneasy so she picked on another topic. 'I had a letter from Sister O'Reilly. She said the mission had a set of extra supplies from the government. She thinks it might have been your influence. Was it?'

He looked embarrassed. 'I was impressed by the work of the mission. I might have dropped a word into the right ear.'

'Even though I'd broken your leg?'

'I try to keep professional decisions separate from personal feelings,' he said tightly.

It wasn't like her to feel such emotion, but she had to say it. 'Dr James, I think you're a good, good man,' she whispered. 'And I mean that as a compliment.' She blushed.

There was silence for a while. She forced herself to look at him. He had an odd, abstracted expression, as if his mind were miles away. Then he smiled, and the brilliance of it warmed her so that she smiled, too.

'Enough of high emotion,' he said. 'This has been a hard day. I had to come to see you and I would have brought you flowers or a bottle but I was past thinking. So I'll say goodnight and...' He climbed painfully to his feet.

'I've got a bottle,' she said. 'Can we drink some of it as a peace offering?'

He looked at her and sat down again. 'I'd like that,' he said.

She went on, 'You've eaten all my biscuits—and you're very welcome. But I think you're hungry. Can I do you cheese on toast?'

'Nurse Grey, you're unbelievable. I'd love cheese on toast. I'm ravenous.'

She fetched a bottle of red wine that had been given

to her by a grateful mum on the south coast. He looked at it approvingly. 'Do you always drink this?'

'No. It was a gift.' She explained the circumstances, then went to make toast, grate cheese and make a quick side salad. He ate happily as they had a more general conversation, skating round topics best ignored. She found she was enjoying his company no end—but, then, she always had.

She took away his plate when he had finished, smiling at his obviously sincere compliments. It was an easy, friendly evening. After the high drama of their early conversation they needed to relax. Then she reached over to take his glass just as he reached for it. Their fingers met and both laughed a little but neither pulled away. His hand slid over hers, imprisoning it gently, and pulled her towards him. She could easily have released herself, but she didn't.

The coffee-table lay between them—he was sitting on the couch and she on an easy chair. It seemed the most natural thing in the world for her to walk around and sit by his side. His grip was very light. She could break away if she wished, but she didn't.

They now sat side by side, and she turned to gaze at him. What could she read in his eyes? They were dark, but in their depths she felt she could read what he thought, know what he was feeling.

With a sigh she closed her own eyes and leaned back. Her body seemed powerless. She wanted to take, not give.

He kissed her. It was the gentlest of kisses, his lips barely grazing hers, a touch as light as air. But, oh, so sweet. He put his arm around her and rested his cheek against hers. She could feel the slight roughness of his chin and the warmth of his breath in her hair. And there was the feel of his body against hers. That, too, was warm.

At first it seemed so restful, just lying there and doing nothing. But slowly his closeness worked his magic on her. As if possessed of a mind of their own, her arms rose and wrapped around him. Their bodies pressed together more tightly.

He kissed her again. It was still a slow, exploratory caress, but her body had told him that it wanted more. His tongue slid round her lips, teasing and tantalising, unbearably provocative. Her hand moved round his neck, pulling him closer.

She hadn't felt like this for so long. She knew nothing but the joy of being with him, of being close to him. She wanted to give all of her being to him.

Now his kiss was passionate, demanding, an emblem of the feelings that they shared. His hand slipped inside the front of her gown, easing the edges apart as he reached for her breast. She thrilled at his touch, the hardness of her nipples betraying her longing.

They were in no hurry. He eased aside her gown and tugged gently at her nightie, his hands reaching inside to hold her more fully. She sighed again. This was bliss. She was being carried along on a tide of sensuality, its speed slowly accelerating until she... Until she what?

With infinite sadness she took her arms from round him and gently eased him away. 'I think we should stop there,' she whispered.

He took a deep, deep breath. 'I will, if that's what you want,' he said. Only the slightest tremor in his voice told her what it was costing him.

'It's not what I want,' she said fretfully, 'but there's more to me than just my body. There are, well, things you don't know about.'

'Are you frightened of me?' he asked reproachfully.

'No, no,' she assured him. 'I'm frightened of myself. You've started feelings in me that have been dead for more than two years. I don't know how to cope. I don't know if I can cope. Stephen, do you mind if I ask you to go?'

He managed to smile, but she could sense the tension behind it. 'I'll go, Emily, but I'll be coming back some time.' She knew he didn't just mean coming to her flat.

At her door he turned to kiss her again, lightly, like a friend. 'When will I see you again?' he asked.

'I'll be at work tomorrow.' She knew that wasn't what he'd meant.

Impatiently he said, 'Emily, you know there's something between us. You can't ignore it and it won't go away. And it's driving me mad.'

'I know,' she said quietly. 'Stephen, it's hard for me, too, but will you give me time?'

He kissed her again, quickly. 'I'll give you time. But not a lot.' Then he was gone.

Mechanically she went to the kitchen to wash up. Now what have you done? she asked herself. And the answer came—whatever it was, you enjoyed it. The next question followed inevitably. So what are you *going* to do? That was harder to answer.

CHAPTER SEVEN

'HAVE you got a minute, Emily?' The speaker was a red-faced, rather embarrassed-looking Denise Coles, who asked her the question as she came on for her early shift next morning.

'Of course,' Emily said warily. She'd forgotten about the treatment she'd received on the ward the previous day—she'd had too much else to think about. Now she remembered.

'Yesterday I accused you of making a dangerous mistake with your patient. Now I know it wasn't your fault, I accused you unjustly. Emily, I'm sorry.'

Emily heaved a sigh of relief. 'Forget it,' she said cheerfully. 'You were only doing your job.'

'I can't forget it. I know how I'd feel if I were accused of something like that. I should have known better.'

'Really,' Emily reassured her, 'I don't mind. I'm just glad it's been sorted out. Er—how did you find out so quickly?'

'Dr James phoned me at home. Normally he wouldn't bother staff when they're off duty, but I'm glad he did this time.'

'So I'm off time-wasting duties?' Emily asked with a grin. 'I can mix with real mums-to-be again?'

Denise turned redder than ever. 'You certainly can. In fact, I'm putting you in with a problem case. I know you can handle it.' She scowled. 'I think the least said the better, but I will tell you that Dr Taylor is off on sick leave. She'd better not come back onto *my* ward.'

'Quite,' said Emily. It was good to have things settled.

Five minutes later she was walking down the corridor with Kathy, discussing what Denise had called a problem case. As with so many of their cases, this was a personal problem rather than a medical one.

'Mum-to-be is April Flowers,' Kathy said.

'Honestly?' Emily couldn't believe it.

'Honestly. I gather her mother was a sixties hippie, and April is still carrying a lot of her ideas. She's a primigravida, and came swanning in early this morning because her waters had broken. No doubt about what she wanted. ''I refuse to have any pain relief. I want to experience childbirth to the full—the bonding will be greater between my partner, myself and our baby. I've brought my oil of almond and my tapes of whale song. They will help me through.'''

'And?' queried Emily with a smile.

'Well, we gave up on the pain-relief-free labour an hour ago. She had diamorphine. The oil of almond and the whale song didn't work. I'm afraid April's having rather a bad time. She's not dilating, not progressing at all. Baby's head is still minus three above the spines. But the CTG has been great and variability is fine with no decelerations at all.'

'She's going to need a section?' Emily guessed.

'Well, I think so. So far all our attempts to accelerate labour have failed. We've tried Prostin gel repeatedly, to no effect. I called the house officer a while ago and he thought she might have to have a section, but the partner wouldn't hear of it.'

'The *partner* wouldn't?' Emily was beginning to see why Kathy was so irritated.

'Bearded twit. He dozed for most of the night, then he went out for a smoke, and by the smell of him it wasn't tobacco he was smoking. He talked her into waiting a while. Good luck with the pair of them.'

Emily went into the labour room, smiled at April and introduced herself. She nodded briefly at the husband, who was managing to hold his partner's hand and doze at the same time. There was the sheen of sweat on April's face, and Emily gently wiped it way. Then she sent the husband out of the room while she conducted a swift examination. The head had still not descended.

'It's possible that you may need to think again about having a Caesarean section,' Emily said soberly. 'I appreciate you want a natural childbirth, but there's more than you to think of. There's the baby, too. You don't want to put it at risk and an overlong labour isn't a good idea.' She knew it was a grossly unfair argument but she felt she had to make April realise there were other points of view than those put forward by the 'bearded twit'.

'Is the baby all right?' April gasped, and Emily reassured her.

'A fine healthy heartbeat. I can hear it perfectly. I just want you to know that you have options, that's all. And this is *your* decision. *You're* having the baby.'

'But we're a partnership! We take decisions together.'

'Only you can take decisions about your body. Now, would you like a drink of water?'

Two hours later the contractions were still inadequate and the head was still high. April had had enough. The oil of almond and the whale song still hadn't worked. Emily told April that she was sending for the senior house officer again. Fortunately, the partner had enough sense not to object this time and April was quickly whisked into Theatre. Emily scrubbed up and took her place at the side of the table. Minutes later April produced a fine baby girl.

Emily was ready for her lunch after this. This time when she went down to the canteen she did not hide in a corner. There was no one there she recognised so she collected her salad roll, fruit and tea and sat, alone but quite happy in a window-seat.

Ten minutes later Stephen came in—just like yesterday. He was talking to a young man a little shorter than himself. They loaded their trays and then Stephen saw her, waved and the two walked over.

She had time to register that the young man was extremely handsome, but it was the sight of Stephen that made her heart beat faster and her mouth go dry—that made her feel so strangely excited. Heavens, she'd seen him only last night, but it was lovely to see him again.

'Emily, this is Ben Crosby. May we join you?'

'Of course.' Did he need to ask? Didn't he know what his presence did to her? She smiled and accepted Ben's outstretched hand. Quickly she noted his smart jacket, white shirt and university tie. 'You look just like a television actor,' she said mischievously.

He looked woebegone. 'But I want to look like a doctor. How could you tell I wasn't a doctor?'

'I'm sorry. You do look like a doctor. I'm afraid I've been told about you.' The two men sat, and Stephen looked surprised as Emily explained that Harry Shea, a family friend, had told her Ben would be coming.

'I'm here to get in people's way,' Ben said, 'but the hospital has been very good.'

Emily needed to talk to Ben—it was one way of keeping her attention from Stephen. Just by sitting next to her, Stephen was affecting her, and she was sure people could tell.

'What part are you going to play?' she asked Ben.

'I'm playing a young doctor, inexperienced, skilful at medicine but poor with people. He gets to work in a hospital clinic, and also meets some of his patients socially. The programme will concentrate on problems he faces and the decisions he has to make. We want to show that there's more to being a doctor than simple medical knowledge.'

'Emily will tell you about making decisions,' Stephen said dryly, and she blushed a little, even though she could hear the humour in his voice.

If he can laugh at it then he's forgiven me, she thought. While Ben was looking away she reached under the table and gave Stephen's hand a quick squeeze. He looked at her inscrutably.

'I know it's only a soap,' Ben went on, 'but millions of people watch soaps. It must have an effect. And I want it to be the right one.'

Emily was suddenly aware that she was unusually popular. People she knew only vaguely were smiling at her, saying hello, stopping for the odd word. People she didn't know were passing the table very slowly. She grinned at Ben. 'Are you being recognised?' she asked.

He turned slightly red. 'Well, I was in another soap for a while. I was a teenager in *Landon's Gate*. People remember the face, even if they can't remember where from.'

She thought she liked him. He was enthusiastic but also genuinely modest. She liked people who were enthusiastic. 'I think I watched it when I was younger,' she said. 'You had longer hair then.'

He nodded. 'You don't want a doctor with long hair.' He stood. 'I'm going to get myself another cup of tea. Anyone else want anything?'

Both Stephen and Emily wanted more tea. 'I'll fetch it,' Emily suggested, but he shook his head decisively.

'This is work for me. You'd be surprised at the ideas you can pick up in queues.' He walked away gracefully. Emily grinned as she saw heads turn to follow him. It was like wind, blowing through a field of wheat.

Now she and Stephen were alone together—apart, that was, from the two hundred or so other people in the canteen. They looked at each other, he gravely, she apprehensively.

'You told the sister about Lyn,' she said. 'There was no need. I meant it when I said I'd take the blame.'

'I know you did, but I thought it wrong. Anyway, Sister and I decided to keep it quiet.' She could feel the touch of steel in his voice again. He went on, 'And

I did take your advice. Lyn's going to see a psychiatrist and I won't report her to the G.M.C. We've also
arranged a transfer to another hospital for her after
she's had a break. I suppose I can feel a bit sorry for
her now.'

'And a bit guilty?' Emily probed.

He looked at her thoughtfully. 'Do you think I
should I feel guilty?'

'Only you know what you should feel.'

'You're a hard woman, Nurse Grey. Yes, I do feel
a bit guilty. Of a lack of perception, if nothing else.
I should have known what she was feeling for me.
But I really didn't know, Emily.'

'I believe you,' she said gently.

'Anyway...there are more important things we
have to talk about. More pleasant things. Like last
night.'

She looked nervously over at the queue, but there
was no chance of Ben rejoining them for a while. The
queue, in fact, seemed not to have moved at all since
Ben joined it.

Her voice was soft. 'I wouldn't want you to think
that I behave like that with just anyone,' she said.

'I don't. And that you feel that you can be like that
with me—well, I'm more pleased than I can say.'

She lowered her head. 'I acted like that because...because I wanted to.'

He took her confession with the seriousness she had
intended. 'Have we started something?' he asked
gently. 'I think we have, and I think you know it, too.
It began in Africa the minute I saw you.'

'Yes,' she agreed, almost reluctantly, 'but there are
things I've not told you yet, and I'm still a bit uncer-

tain. I've got so used to…keeping things to myself
that I'm, well, I'm a bit scared.'

He nodded gently. 'We all have secrets. Tell you
what, let me take you to dinner. You know me well
enough by now to know I won't push you into anything you don't want.'

Her smile was tentative. 'Just being with you
pushes me, Stephen. At the moment I don't think I
can cope. I won't go to dinner with you. I'm still…'
She couldn't find words to finish the sentence.

He understood. 'You're the Bogart film expert.
Remember that film with Lauren Bacall where she
tells him that all he has to do is whistle? Well, that's
how I'll be. Whistle when you want me. But don't
wait too long.'

'I'll try not to.' She decided that she had talked
enough about her feelings for a while. Lunchtime in
the middle of a crowded canteen wasn't the time or
place to have an emotional conversation. 'Serious
talking makes me dry,' she said with a shaky laugh.
'Where's my cup of tea?'

Both turned, then smiled at each other. Ben was
now firmly surrounded by an admiring group. 'You're
going to be the most popular woman in hospital,'
Stephen said mischievously. 'You're taking him up to
your ward. Introduce him to Denise. He's going to
play a gynaecologist.'

'I'll sell tickets,' she said dryly.

Later on, when she had a quiet moment, she wondered why she'd turned down Stephen's invitation to
dinner. She liked him, she trusted him and he made
her feel as no man had for a very long time. But there

was still a deadweight on her life, something that warned her never to trust a man again.

She was walking down the corridor, and on impulse she pushed open the door to a room where a mother and her new baby were both resting. She looked down at the little scrap of humanity, clad in its hospital gown, lying in its clear plastic cot. The tiny face seemed utterly content. Even now, after two years in Africa and after she had helped so many babies into the world, she still occasionally felt a pang, like a knife in the heart. She smiled reassuringly at the mother, who had turned her head to look at her. 'Lovely baby,' she said, and walked out.

She wasn't quite sure what kind of relationship Stephen wanted with her but, from her knowledge of his character, she suspected it would be a serious one. He'd want things she didn't think she could give. Shiny-eyed, she went back to her work.

At home that night, just as she was thinking about the previous evening, her phone rang. It was Ben. He'd been with her for quite a while that afternoon. She'd introduced him to patients as well as staff. When they'd learned who he was and what he wanted, the patients were only too pleased to co-operate. Everyone wanted to help make a TV soap. And Ben was so good with them. Emily thought he was a kind, considerate man.

'I learned a lot, Emily,' he said. 'I enjoyed the day and I'm looking forward to coming in again next week. But that's not why I rang. I want to do something in return. I understand you're off work in a couple of days. Would you like to come over and see how we make a programme?'

By now Emily was an avid television fan, and she'd told him so. And she especially liked soaps. 'You mean, see it actually being acted? I'd love to come and watch,' she said eagerly.

'Good. I've fixed it with the director. Normally we don't like visitors on the set, but you've been good to us so we'd like to be good to you. Turn up about nine in the morning and give your name to the gate-man. Do you know where the studio is?'

'I know where it is and I'll be there early,' she promised.

She quite liked Ben. He was gentle and undemanding. He'd be a good friend.

It was interesting to watch the programme being recorded. She sat at the back of a large gallery with the director, secretaries and technicians in front of her. There was an array of flickering television screens. Below them, through a great window, was the set of a street corner. She recognised it, but now she could see that the buildings were backless and constructed of wood. There were cameras, lights and cables threaded along the road.

It reminded her of the scene in a hospital theatre—apparently chaotic, but everyone knowing their own particular job.

Ben sat by her for much of the time, introducing her to people as someone who was helping him. She was made to feel welcome, and when she left she said quite honestly that she'd thoroughly enjoyed herself.

He smiled at her. 'So may I take you to dinner tonight, then?' He looked anxious as he waited for her reply—and that decided her.

'I'd love to come to dinner. But, Ben, you know how Harry Shea has a relationship with my sister? They're just friends. Well, that's the only kind of relationship I'm interested in right now. There have been things in my past I'm not yet over. I wouldn't want to...want you to get the wrong idea.'

'You'll change in time,' he said comfortingly. 'The pain will ease.' She coloured.

He went on, 'Emily, I just want your company, that's all. If I wanted anything else, well, I had two offers from nurses last week.'

'I'm ashamed of my hospital,' she said cheerfully. 'Earthy types, us nurses.'

'Pick you up at half past seven?'

'I'm looking forward to it.' She gave him her address.

That's two offers of dinner in a week, she realised as she drove away from the studio. And I've not accepted the one from the man I care for most. Still, I enjoy Ben's company.

Ben called for her in his car that evening and took her out to the moors to the east of town. They had dinner in a pub, sitting in the garden and eating home-made pie and salad.

'This isn't what I expected,' she said. 'I thought television actors led exciting lives and you'd take me somewhere super-sophisticated.'

He blushed. 'I'm sorry. I thought you'd like it here,' he said.

She realised he was genuinely upset. Leaning over, she pushed him on the shoulder. 'Of course I like it here, idiot. And I like being with you. It's just that I have these foolish ideas about what an actor's life is like. Come on, tell me about it. Is there as much hard work as glamour?'

He relaxed. 'There's not a lot of glamour, being an actor in a soap. Even opening supermarkets is hard work. But I enjoy it.' He went on to tell her about the long hours, the waiting and the difficulty of having anything like a social life when you were acting in something that went out twice a week. She was fascinated.

There were other people, having their meal in the garden. Nearest was a family with two teenagers. The girl noticed Ben first. Their conversation died as she whispered to each in turn. Then the family, in an elaborately casual manner, each had a long look at Ben.

'You've been spotted,' Emily whispered.

He grinned ruefully. 'It's the price you pay. It won't be the first time.'

The family waited until Emily and Ben were having coffee, then the girl came over. 'You're Ben Crosby,' she said shyly. 'I saw you in *Landon's Gate.*'

'That's right. But it was a couple of years ago— it's nice to be remembered. What's your name?'

The girl introduced herself but it was obvious that, although she was thrilled, she had no real idea what she wanted to ask. After a few minutes of stilted conversation and the promise of a posted photograph she fled back to her family, and shortly after that they left. They all waved, and Ben waved back.

'Do you get much of that kind of thing?' Emily asked curiously.

He shrugged. 'Quite a bit. There'll be more when I start this new part.'

'Do you mind?'

'At times it can be a bit irritating. Sometimes it's great fun. But these people, in effect, pay me so I feel they're entitled to think I'm some kind of friend. But—don't hit me if I say it—every now and then it's nice to have an ordinary relationship. Like I'm having with you.'

She laughed. 'And I thought I was an extraordinary woman. You disappoint me.' She enjoyed being with him. She felt unthreatened but happy to be in male company. He was witty and charming, and she was certainly rather pleased to be seen out with such a handsome man. But he was no threat. For some reason, when she thought of him and Stephen there was just no comparison.

He asked her about life on the ward. His questions were pointed and intelligent and made her rethink some of her attitudes. When they finally left she felt she'd had a good evening and had made a new friend.

He kissed her goodnight but it was an affectionate kiss, not a demanding one. He made it clear that he didn't expect to be asked into her flat—for coffee or anything else. She realised she was getting more and more relaxed in male company, but was she ready yet for the intensity of a relationship with Stephen? She didn't know. And if she wasn't certain then she wouldn't start.

She was now well into the swing of work in the ward. If anything, it was too easy. In Africa there had never been enough time or enough resources. Here she had a vast back-up of expertise and technology to help her if she had the slightest problem. It was good for the mums and babies, of course, but she wasn't stretched as much as she used to be. Perhaps that was a good thing. No longer at night did she agonise over whether she'd made the right decision.

She saw Stephen several times in the next week—but always professionally, always with someone else present. He greeted her cordially, as he did all the staff. He was friendly and well liked, but she knew that there was an extra feeling for her. His gaze lingered on her just a little longer than was necessary and his body seemed to be closer to hers than it needed to be. And she loved it.

The warm days of summer were coming closer. One day, after she'd finished her shift and was walking through the hospital car park, she saw him. He was leaning against his car, looking casual in a crisp, blue, short-sleeved shirt and grey trousers. Her memory went back to when she'd first seen him in the mountains, so many hundreds of miles away in Africa. He'd looked attractive then, too.

She was improving. She was able to smile at him and demonstrate simple pleasure at meeting a friend and a colleague. But what she showed was nothing like the turmoil of what she was feeling.

'What a gorgeous day.' It was the kind of casual greeting that friends gave each other.

'Certainly is.' The smile he returned was deceptively casual. 'I was waiting for you, Emily.'

That she hadn't expected. 'Any special reason?' she asked cautiously.

'I wanted to talk to you. And I'm tired of playing

doctor-nurse games on the ward. Have you got an hour now?'

She had but did she want to spend it talking to him? For a moment she looked at him in silence. Perhaps there were more lines at the corners of his eyes. He looked tired, but being tired was common for a specialist registrar.

'I'm not doing anything at all this evening,' she said.

'Good. I've got to pick something up from the office and then I'm free for a while. You know the car park on the beach by your flat?'

She did know it. She often walked on the long stretch of grass there. Because it was still in suburbia, it didn't get too crowded.

'I know it,' she acknowledged.

'I'll see you by the ice-cream kiosk. In about fifteen minutes?'

'I'll be there.' The decision had been made. She walked to the little car she'd been borrowing from Lisa.

There were benches, facing the sea, near the kiosk. She picked one where she'd be obvious and sat, watching the sea. The sun shone, turning the sea into a hot blue mirror. A couple of cargo ships chugged slowly down the estuary. She liked it here.

'You make me do mad things, Emily.'

He'd come up behind her, unobserved. In fact, she'd deliberately not looked for him. She'd wanted his arrival to be a surprise. And it was!

He leaned over and presented her with an ice-cream cornet. But what a cornet! 'What's this?' she gasped.

He moved round to sit by her. 'It's one vanilla, one

chocolate and one strawberry scoop. There are hundreds and thousands scattered on top and two chocolate bars stuck in. I turned down the rasberry cordial. Didn't want to seem excessive, you know.'

'Such delicacy. Stephen, this looks absolutely mouth-watering.'

'I've got plain vanilla. I thought you still needed feeding up a bit. Go on, try it?'

She did. If anything, it tasted better than it looked. 'Alberto's got a reputation for ice cream,' she mumbled, trying to lick a stray chocolate crumb from the side of her mouth.

'It's deserved. Emily, I love the way your tongue flicks in and out.'

'It's all your fault. And it's probably a strawberry-coloured tongue right now.'

'True. Shall we send you up to Infectious Diseases? I think you've got pellagra.'

'A deficiency of nicotinic acid,' she recalled aloud. 'I've seen a couple of cases of it in Africa.'

'Me, too.' They sat in silence for a moment. He *is* sensitive, she thought. He's put me at my ease, made me relax. I like him. And the ice cream is wonderful.

His mood changed, his voice becoming more serious. 'I've hardly seen you for a fortnight,' he said, 'I was hoping you'd phone me. I've missed you.'

'You've seen me on the ward,' she pointed out.

'Not the same. I think you're trying to avoid me, Emily.'

It was the time for absolute honesty. 'I *am* avoiding you. It hurts, but you frighten me, Stephen.'

She could hear the distress in his voice. 'I don't mean to frighten you. It's the last thing I want.'

She had to make it clear what she meant. 'I'm more frightened of me than you. You bring out feelings in me that I can't handle. I just need time.'

'You've been seeing Ben Crosby,' he said quietly.

'I have. Truly, Stephen, he's just a friend. He's helping me get back into a world I left. I can cope with him because he's not a threat.'

'I see.' She knew by the little sigh he gave that she'd convinced him. 'There's something in your past, isn't there, Emily? Something that's marked you, hurt you.'

'Yes.' She couldn't say more than the stark, simple word.

'Will you tell me about it? Telling often helps.'

'I don't think I can. Not yet.'

He persisted gently. 'I suspect it's to do with a crash. I've seen the scars on your abdomen.'

Jerkily she said, 'That's part of it. My sisters know, of course, but you're not to ask them.'

He put out his hand and stroked her shoulder. It was a gesture of his that she'd noted and seen him do to anxious mums. 'I won't try to find out, Emily, but I hope you'll tell me soon.'

She had difficulty speaking but she nodded. 'Soon,' she managed to whisper.

His voice changed back to that of a busy doctor. 'I've got a meeting in ten minutes. I must go. But you know I'm thinking of you, Emily?'

'I know. I'll...try.'

He stood and stooped to kiss her briefly on the cheek. 'Finish your ice cream,' he said, and was gone.

What was she to do? She sat for another hour until the slight breeze from the sea chilled her. Ideas, emotions, long repressed, were coming back to haunt her. Feelings that she'd sworn never to entertain again. But he was such a *good* man. She shivered, and went to drive back to her flat.

Two minutes after she entered her flat the phone rang. It was Ben. 'Getting in touch as early as I can. A fortnight on Saturday is the riverboat cruise. There will be a big group of us. Will you come as my partner? Both your sisters are coming.'

'That would be lovely, Ben,' she said enthusiastically. 'Of course I'll come with you.'

Ben was simple, friendly, no trouble. She liked being with him. But what should she do about Stephen? She made herself confront the fact that she'd never acknowledged to herself. She loved him. But she'd sworn to herself never to fall in love again.

CHAPTER EIGHT

SINCE she was a child Emily had loved dressing up. She'd always enjoyed sewing, and when she had time she liked to make or alter her own clothes. In Africa she'd had plenty of practice. A lot of her clothes had needed to be taken in.

For the riverboat cruise everyone was supposed to dress as a Mississippi gambler or a Southern belle. The ferry was being turned into a Mississippi riverboat. She found pictures in the local library, went round to Lisa's and they both watched *Gone with the Wind* on video. Then she raided the local charity shops, borrowed Lisa's sewing machine and bought herself a big straw hat. It was a different kind of hard work—and she enjoyed it.

Finally she was finished. The Friday night before the cruise she stood in front of her mirror and decided without false modesty that she'd done well.

In Africa she'd always kept her hair short as it was less bother. But since she'd got back to England she'd let it grow longer. On the ward she kept it in a French pleat but for the dance she'd decided to wear it loose, and had spent a happy half-day, experimenting with various styles. Now the rich red tresses curled in ringlets on her shoulders.

Her high-waisted skirt and short jacket were in a dark green velvet, which contrasted with her red hair. The skirt was long and had just the suggestion of a bustle, made by twisting the material at the back of the waistband. She'd made a white silk blouse—and wondered if she'd ever dare to wear it again. It was authentic, but it did show rather a lot of what she learned was called her 'front'. A silk scarf in matching green was wrapped around her hat. Yes, she'd done well.

The cruise was in aid of hospital charities. The charities committee had chartered a ferryboat, which would sail down the river to the bar and back. Tickets were expensive, but much sought after. In the past the cruise had been a great success, and everyone expected it to be the same again.

She was joining a large party. Alex and Lisa were coming, with Harry and Sally Shea. Rosalind was coming but had decided—in spite of being asked by several men—that she didn't want a partner. She herself was going with Ben, and there were a few other people from the hospital or the television series. Emily knew she'd be among friends. And it was years since she'd been to a really good fancy-dress party.

Carefully she unbuttoned the blouse and stepped out of the skirt. Standing there in bra and briefs, she was glad she didn't have to wear the same underclothes as a Southern lady. She'd seen pictures of tightly pinched corsets, of bloomers down to the knee—it must have been intolerable in the humid heat of the American South.

The phone rang. It was Ben. Judging by his rushed words and his agitated tones, he was obviously very upset. 'Emily, really bad news. I'm awfully sorry but I can't make the cruise tomorrow. I've just had a call from London. There's a Dr Goldring in the East End who does just the kind of work I'm supposed to do in the series. He says I can shadow him for a weekend—but it's got to be this weekend. He's going away on Monday. I really can't pass up this chance.'

Emily was calm. 'That's all right, Ben. I'll be with a big party. But I'll miss you.' She felt disappointed, of course, but, she had to admit, only mildly disappointed. And one of the things she liked about Ben was his dedication to his work. He'd do anything to get things right.

'So you don't mind?' Ben asked, relieved.

'Well, of course, I'm sorry you're not coming but I want you to do what's best for your career. I'd do exactly the same. And I should have a good time, anyway.'

'Emily, you're a darling. I'll bring you back a stick of London rock.' He rang off and Emily smiled to herself. What would she have thought if Stephen had broken a date like this? Would she have accepted it so easily? Not that she'd ever had what you might call a date with him.

On Saturday evening she was picked up by a minibus, organised by Alex. He looked dashing in the traditional Mississippi black frock coat, and both her sisters looked well. Lisa had adapted a blue-and-silver-striped evening dress and Rosalind had found a long white dress that made her look demure and sweet—a totally false impression, Emily knew.

A team from the television company had been working on the ferryboat all afternoon. It was amazing what a difference props and swathes of cloth could make. The workaday ferry was gone, and in its place was a set of rooms with mirrors, chandeliers and all the trappings of nineteenth-century graceful living. Emily knew she was going to enjoy herself.

The main room was where the dance would take place, and Alex had reserved a table. Downstairs was a mock gaming room and a buffet.

It was a warm night so when the ferryboat finally slid away from the pier, and the band was still tuning up, Emily climbed upstairs to the top deck.

It was exciting, as boat trips so often were. She watched the great docks slide past and the river traffic, bobbing past them as they made their way out towards the sea. Suddenly she had a sense of her own life as a river, moving inexorably towards—what? Somewhere was there a sea of contentment for her? She wasn't cold, but she shivered and went back downstairs.

The dance was fun. The compère started with comparatively modern music and only when people were obviously enjoying themselves and joining in did he introduce nineteenth-century dancing. Emily enjoyed being bowed to, and curtsying. She now knew quite a few people and danced more or less non-stop.

Alex ordered a couple of bottles of white wine, and she enjoyed a glass. She was amused to hear her fearsome younger sister explain things to an importunate, slightly drunken lecturer. 'No, I will *not* dance with you. You appear incapable of remaining upright. Why don't you go and drink some black coffee?'

Emily winced. What kind of a man would Rosalind find?

It was buffet time. Alex organised his party to go downstairs. 'Lisa has to keep her strength up,' he ex-

plained with a grin. 'She's feeding two, you know.'
Emily was too excited to eat so she excused herself
and went back on the top deck.

'I'm warm,' she said. 'I'll be down with you later.'

She was alone. It was dark now, and only the passing lights hinted at the city on the river bank. She
listened to the thumping of the boat's engines, the
distant hum of conversation and the hiss of water
passing by the keel. It was a moment of peace.

There was the tap of feet on the stairwell behind
her. Thinking it might be Alex or another of her party,
she turned. The deck here was only dimly lit, but she
recognised the swift walk, the angle of head and
shoulder, the broad shoulders. It was Stephen.

For some reason she didn't feel surprised. There
was a sudden burst of hope and anticipation that
frightened her as well as excited her. He was here.
That was all that mattered.

He, too, was dressed in a traditional gambler's outfit, but from somewhere he'd found a frock coat in a
rich burgundy. The ornate outfit only complemented
his masculinity. Not every man could get away with
wearing a frilled shirt like that, she thought. He looks
tougher than normal—almost frightening.

When she thought about it she was surprised to see
him. She'd told him she was going to be here with
Ben. He'd said gloomily that three was a crowd so he
wouldn't come.

'I didn't expect to see you here,' she said frankly.

He joined her at the rail. 'I was offered a ticket
yesterday, and decided to come then.'

A ship passed them, heading upriver, and both
paused to watch it. 'I wanted to see you away from

the hospital again,' he went on, 'but when you were with friends.'

'That's thoughtful of you,' she said. 'I'd like to say it's not necessary, that I'm not frightened of you, but it's not entirely true.'

'I don't want to frighten you,' he said gently.

She nodded. 'I know that, Stephen.' She decided to change the mood. 'How come I've not seen you so far? You could have asked me for a dance.'

'I hope to later. I've been downstairs, having a boring conversation with a boring millionaire. He's thinking of giving the hospital a donation so I suppose it's worth it.'

He turned towards her, and even in the half-light she could see the sheepish expression in his eyes. 'Better get it over with quickly. Emily, I've got a confession to make.'

'Go on.' Somehow she didn't think it would be too terrible.

'Your actor friend, Ben, isn't here?'

'No. He got the chance of shadowing a doctor in London. It's just what he wants, just the kind of work he's supposed to be doing in the series. He's very conscientious, you know. What confession?'

Stephen coughed. 'Ben asked me if I knew anyone suitable. I said I'd ask around and then he received a phone call from a Dr David Goldring, a very old friend of mine. I'm afraid I arranged for Ben to be called away.'

'You did what?' She couldn't believe it, it was just too comic.

'I wanted to see you so I did something that was

low, underhand, childish and irresponsible. And I'm not the least bit sorry.'

'What about poor Ben?'

'Well, I have arranged with David that he sees everything that he wants to. Ben will have a profitable weekend.' Slyly, he added, 'All I did was make a decision for you.'

'Ouch,' she said. 'I suppose I deserved that.'

He shook his head. 'I'm not a vindictive person. Are you going to forgive me?'

'I think you should ask Ben that. But, yes, I am.' She felt rather flattered that he'd gone to such trouble just to see her. 'Did you want to see me for any special reason?'

'Only one reason. And that's special to me. I've been looking at you from the bar. I've never seen you together with your sisters. Grey is the completely wrong name for three such exciting women. Couldn't you be called Titian or something?'

'No. I've seen Titian's women. They're all a bit big for me.'

She shivered, again not through the cold. 'D'you want my coat?' he asked, and when she shook her head he put his arm round her instead. She leaned against him.

It was inevitable that he would kiss her. She moved happily in his arms, reaching round inside his coat to hug the oak-like strength of him. She could stay here for ever, alone on this deck with this man. She felt her need for him as she recognised his need for her. And flooding from the past came memories of the last time she had given way so completely—and the agony it had caused her.

Could she go through with that again? Gently she
pushed him away, then rested her head on his shoulder. It wasn't kissing, was it?

She wasn't surprised when she realised he'd recognised her mood, almost read her mind. 'Tell me,' he
said gently. And suddenly she realised she would. She
had to now.

Her emotions were getting out of control with this
man. He wasn't amiable, easily directed, like Ben. She
looked down at the black water, flowing past. If she
dived into it could she swim to the shore? Falling for
Stephen would be just as dangerous.

It would be best to tell him quickly, while she felt
she could. Jerkily, she began. 'I have to distrust
men—and my feelings. I'm not the tough, competent,
hard midwife you think you know.'

He interrupted. 'I think you're tough and you're
competent. But never have I thought you were hard.'

'You know how I like my own way? To take other
people's decisions?'

She tried to make it a joke. He didn't. 'I recognise
nothing will stop you from doing what you think is
best,' he said. 'And you're ready to take the consequences.'

'Consequences,' she repeated. Her voice was bitter.
'I know all about consequences.

'I was the middle daughter. We were a loving family—we still are—but I had no mother that I can remember, and perhaps that made me a bit wild.
Anyway, I qualified as a nurse, then went straight into
midwife training. That's how it used to be done. I
loved being a midwife. Halfway through my training
I met a young doctor, Allan Tye, a house officer on

my ward. We fell for each other, like you do at that age. And I was young.'

She paused, then drove herself on. Stephen knew better than to interrupt.

'My love for him was everything to me, and nothing else in the world mattered. My family suggested caution, patience—why not wait a while? We were both working hard, starting our careers. But, no, we had to get married. And we did.

'We set up house in a tiny flat, and for eight weeks I was deliriously happy. And then the trouble started. Allan came home, ranting about how the consultant on his ward was old, incompetent and shouldn't be in charge of anyone. This amazed me because I knew the man and I knew that he was good. So I asked Allan what had happened, and it turned out that he had been neglecting his duty and been told off.

'When I suggested that he was being unfair to the consultant he told me I was a stupid little midwife who couldn't be expected to understand anything. Then he slammed out of the house and came home some hours later, dead drunk. Allan had fooled me. In fact, he'd fooled the entire family.'

She took a deep breath, aware that her voice was trembling. 'My husband was a drunken weakling. He couldn't take responsibility. He couldn't even handle contraception, as he'd said he would. A fortnight after this I found out I was pregnant.'

There was silence again as she relived those evil days—and the last one the most evil of all.

'But I was determined that, if possible, I was going to make the marriage work. I was not going to abandon everything as my mother had done. I'd be strong enough for both of us. So we carried on, with me doing my job, and he making a mess of his.'

She hoped she had the strength to get through the rest of the story. Usually, whenever she thought of it, she wept. But it had to be told.

'We'd been to a hospital party. As ever, he'd had too much to drink. I said I'd drive home and he fell asleep. I was six months pregnant.'

'He woke up after I'd driven a while and said he wanted to feel his baby. *His* baby! Before I knew what he was doing he'd unfastened my safety belt. And he'd unfastened his own. He fell against me and grabbed the steering-wheel. We were only doing about thirty miles an hour, but we drove straight into a brick wall.

'He was thrown through the windscreen. He broke his neck and died instantly. I was stopped by the steer-ing-wheel. It...it broke and stuck into me. The fire brigade had to cut me out. I had an emergency lapa-rotomy in A and E but my baby was dead. They wanted to get me into Intensive Care as quickly as possible as I'd lost a lot of blood. The cuts in my abdomen were stitched up quickly—the surgeon didn't have time to do a really good job. I was sup-posed to go back to hospital for further surgery to clean them up but I never bothered.'

It was nearly over now. 'It was a long time before I recovered. I developed a pelvic infection. But when I did get better I applied for a job—anywhere far away. I finished up in Africa. So there are two things you need to know about me. I distrust myself because of the mistake I made. I can't tell a good man from

a bad one. I'm not going through that agony again.
And I think probably I'll never have babies.'

The tears were running down her face now. He
pulled her close to him, but said nothing. She was
glad about that. After all, there wasn't much he could
say that would help.

After a while she eased away from him, accepted
the proffered handkerchief and wiped her eyes. 'I
need to go to the Ladies',' she said, 'and make a few
running repairs. After that I'd better rejoin my party.
They'll be wondering where I've got to.'

'I'm on my own,' he said. 'May I join you? Will
anyone mind?'

She was certain of the answer. 'Please do join us.
They'll all be glad to see you. But now I must look
a mess, and I want to put things right.'

She knew he was looking at her, but because of the
darkness she couldn't make out his expression. 'The
misery is now over,' he said thoughtfully. 'You can
now put on a good face. You're in charge again.'

'That's right. I'm midwife Emily Grey. I can cope,
I always do.'

'I see.' Like her, he'd obviously decided to change
his mood. 'Come on, I'm going to be one of those
uncomfortable-looking men you see waiting outside
ladies' cloakrooms.' He took her arm and led her to
the stairs.

The rest of the evening was enjoyable. Stephen was
welcomed by the others, as Emily had known he
would be. Only her two sisters guessed she had been
upset. Emily knew this by the assessing glance that
Lisa gave her. But she thought the evening went well.

Later on the usually silent Rosalind joined her in

the Ladies again. 'I like him,' she said abruptly. 'Why don't you take a chance, sister mine?'

'What d'you mean?' Emily wondered how many other people were going to guess exactly what she was thinking.

'You know very well what I mean. It's obvious that the man is besotted with you. Life moves on, Emily. You've got to join it.'

Rosalind added another touch to her already perfect face. 'Must go. I've got to dance with the cardiac consultant.'

Emily blinked. Why couldn't she run her life with precision like Rosalind apparently did?

She wasn't able to say much to Stephen at the end of the evening. He had ordered a taxi and she was to travel in the minibus, organised by Alex. Briefly he squeezed her hand, that was all. Perhaps it was a good thing. She'd had enough emotion for one night. But she knew she'd started something, rather than bringing it to an end.

He phoned the next morning. She felt both shy and excited when she heard him but then a vicious inner voice reminded her that this was just like being in love.

His voice was tense. Unusually for him, he didn't seem sure of something. And there was no reference to the happy time they'd had the night before. 'Remember once you said that you owed me a favour— all I had to do was ask?'

'Yes,' she answered, her voice cautious, fearful even.

'Well, there is something you can do for me.'

'All right. What is it?'

'I can't tell you over the phone. Look, I'm on my way into hospital—there's a birth I need to be present at in a couple of hours. Can you meet me on the same seat on the front?'

She was dressed, she had the time and she was curious. 'I'll be there,' she said. 'You've intrigued me now. Can't you give me a hint?'

'It's something I have to ask face to face. In about fifteen minutes?'

'That's fine. And no ice cream this time!' But he'd rung off. She reached for her shoes.

He was already waiting when she reached the bench. Today he was dressed casually in a polo shirt and jeans, a contrast from the finery of the night before. She sat by him.

'We were out there last night,' he said, nodding towards the channel. 'It seems a long time ago—not a few hours.'

'I enjoyed it.' She was determined to remember the dancing and the company, not the memories she'd had to rake over when they were on the top deck together. 'You sounded very serious on the phone.'

He looked at her soberly. 'It is something serious, Emily. You said you'd do anything I wanted to make up for breaking my leg. Well, there is something I want. And it's a lot to ask.'

'So ask,' she said cheerfully.

He seemed to change the subject. 'You know my father is Gilbert James, a top obstetrician who special-ises in infertility?'

She did know. 'You told me. Funny that you both specialised in the same field.'

'Yes. Emily, last night you told me about your ac-

cident. Obviously the A and E surgeon was more concerned about making sure you survived than ensuring
you could have children later. Before any really detailed examination you set off for Africa.'

Now she was as unsmiling as he was. 'I'm all right.
I was fit to work abroad.'

'There are different kinds, different levels, of fit-
ness. Emily, I want my father to examine you. To find
out if there's any definite reason why you can't have
children.'

'No!' The answer was automatic, unhesitating. That
was something she just wouldn't think about.

'Why not? You claim to be tough. You should be
tough enough to take what he says.'

She was agitated. 'I am tough. But it's my body,
and any decisions about it I'll take.'

'Decisions' had been the wrong word to use. He
looked at her and said, 'This is my body. Because of
someone else's decision I'll never play rugby again.'

'That's cruel,' she cried.

'It might be cruel but it's true. And I've learned to
live with it, to accept it. Now, are you going to do
this thing for me?' He was inexorable.

'Why do you want to interfere?'

'My reasons are my own. Will you do it?'

There was nowhere else for her to go, no argument
she could think of. 'Yes, I'll do it,' she said.

'Good.' He wasn't going to give her time to change
her mind or to think about what she'd agreed to. 'My
father's coming over tomorrow to spend a few days
in the area. I'll arrange for him to see you at the hospital next Wednesday or Thursday in the evening.'

It was all happening too quickly. 'But—' she protested.

'If you've made up your mind we need to move at once. No time for apprehension, for thinking again.' He unbent a little. 'You'll like my dad. He's not in the least like me.'

'That's a relief,' she muttered. 'I don't think I could manage two of you.'

'It's settled, then. I'd better get into hospital, but I'll be in touch to finalise the arrangement later.' He stood. 'Oh, and, Emily. You made a gorgeous Southern belle.' He stooped to kiss her briefly on the cheek. Then he was gone.

She sat, staring at the sea as if its grey surface could give her the answer to a question she couldn't even ask herself. Why did he want her to know if she could have children?

Stephen had been right. Gilbert James wasn't in the least like his son. He was short, for a start. But there was something in the alertness of his eyes and the way he bounded about the room that reminded her of Stephen.

She'd had many examinations before, and had helped with hundreds. She had already provided a blood sample. But she was still rather apprehensive. I should be able to reassure myself, she thought bleakly. After all, I've reassured many women in my time.

She was surprised when she got to the little examination room, far from her own ward. 'I've persuaded the sister to make us some real coffee,' Dr

James said, 'so pour yourself a cup and come and tell me about Africa.'

So she did. For over twenty minutes she talked about her experiences, gently pushed by his questions. She knew, of course, that he was trying to put her at her ease, but he was also obviously genuinely interested in what she had to say.

He didn't pretend that she was just another patient. 'My son tells me that you're a friend of his. And, like so many midwives, you haven't had time to look after yourself properly. I'm afraid there are a lot of medical people like that. Now, I've had your notes sent up from Shropshire. You did make a mess of yourself, didn't you? Tell me, how long afterwards was it before you felt you were back to normal?'

He carried on with the seemingly gentle conversation—about Africa, about life with her sisters, even about her marriage. She began to realise what a brilliant doctor he was. Through his casual questions he was drawing out all sorts of details about her that she would never have volunteered. And it was all done so pleasantly.

She remembered an occasion the previous week when she was with a young house officer who was clerking a young mum. The house officer was embarrassed and the mum could see his embarrassment. It made things worse. With Dr James it was so easy. She found herself happily telling him about her erratic periods, her occasional panic attacks.

Finally she went behind the screen to take off her tights, then came and climbed onto the examination couch. He looked at her scars first, then gave her a gentle internal examination. It was all so easy.

When she was dressed again he poured her another coffee and said, 'Well, you know we don't usually test for infertility until the couple in question have tried for quite some time. In your case, of course, that doesn't apply.'

'No,' said Emily, feeling vaguely warm.

'Quite. There are a few more tests I'd like to make, but I'm going to stick my neck out. There is almost certainly no reason why you could not have children. I see your original surgeon recommended plastic surgery for the scars on your abdomen, but suggested there was no great hurry. Before it could be done you'd gone to Africa. You refused the treatment.'

With this kind man she felt she could confess, explain. 'I'd lost my baby,' she said.

He knew at once what she meant. 'You felt guilty. I'm not going to tell you that was foolish, I think it was very understandable.'

He pursed his lips. 'The relationship between mind and body is still not fully understood, but they are connected closely. I think you should have your scars removed. I can organise it quite easily. You may then feel a certain…easing of your spirit.'

'All right,' she said after a pause. 'I'll have it done.'

'Good. I'll make arrangements tomorrow.' He poured himself another coffee and beamed at her.

Uncertainly she asked, 'You know your son arranged this?'

'Yes. No problem about it. In a year or two I shall be referring cases to him. He's going to be a very competent gynaecologist.' He smiled the smile of a proud father.

'You know I'm not his patient. I'm his…friend.

Are you going to tell him what you've found and suggested?'

He looked appalled. 'Certainly not. As you say, he's not your doctor.'

Emily swallowed. 'I'd like you to tell him.'

'Hmm. I can if you want. Are you sure you don't want to tell him yourself?'

'No, I'd rather you told him.'

He peered at her shrewdly. 'I take it from this that there is some personal feeling involved?'

She blushed. 'There might be. Some time.'

'Well, I will tell him, if that's what you want.' He gave her a big smile that reminded her very much of Stephen. 'One of the big pleasures of my job is that every now and then I can give people good news. And I *do* enjoy it.'

She didn't see Stephen for another two days. She was on lates and he was working at a clinic in another part of the city. She phoned him, feeling that she had to thank him, but all she got was his answering machine so she mumbled that she'd called to say thanks.

On the third day, when she was still on lates, he phoned her on the ward. She was tired, she was busy, but her heart thumped when she heard his voice.

'Emily, this has got to be short. Can you come round to my flat when you finish your shift? I can't get out. I'm expecting a phone call from America and I must be in for it. There are a couple of things we have to discuss.'

She didn't hesitate. 'I'll be there,' she said.

'Good. Emily, I think you're lovely. See you.' He rang off.

It was the shortest of calls. But it left her heart singing.

He was dressed in a blue T-shirt and jeans, and his feet were bare but for leather sandals. She hadn't seen him for three days and she'd missed him.

She thought he'd missed her. His face lit up as he opened the door, and, instead of kissing her, he hugged her. 'You told me that your family hugged a lot,' he said. 'I think it's a lovely idea. Come in.'

She stepped inside. She'd visited once before, of course, but this time it was different. He remembered. 'Last time you came you met Dr Taylor. I hope this visit is more pleasant.'

'She wasn't exactly unpleasant,' Emily said carefully. 'Do you know how she is?'

'Receiving treatment. You were right, by the way. The psychiatrist says there should be a place for her in medicine somewhere. After all, she'd passed a lot of exams. Just so long as she doesn't want me to give her a job.' He frowned. 'But let's talk about something a bit more pleasant.'

He took her into his living room. She'd liked it before, but now she had a chance to appreciate it. It was graceful but comfortable, with little untidyness that indicated that someone actually lived there.

'You've just finished lates?' he questioned. 'You must be hungry, I've done you a sandwich. I remember you doing me cheese on toast. Sit down and relax. I'll be two minutes in the kitchen.'

He disappeared through a half-open door. 'Can I put on a CD?' she called.

'Whatever you like,' a voice came back. 'The rack's there.'

She picked Gershwin's *Slaughter on Tenth Avenue*. The quirky rhythm had always excited her. Then, as the jerky notes swung around her, she sat on his couch and waited. What did he want with her?

She might have guessed that he was a good sand-wich-maker. He brought in a tray. There were warmed crusty rolls, fresh ham, a soft French cheese and a bowl of tossed salad. There was also a frosted bottle of white wine. He opened it and filled two glasses.

'This, Dr James, looks like the setting for a seduc-tion,' she said pertly as she accepted a glass.

'Don't think I hadn't considered it, but I've got even more important things to talk to you about. Now, you eat and I'll tell you why I've asked you to come here.'

'Sounds important,' she managed to say around a mouthful of ham sandwich. She hadn't realised how ravenous she was.

'The first thing is that I'm going to Chicago—early tomorrow. I'll be away for three months.'

Suddenly she wasn't happy any more. 'That's a bit sudden, isn't it?' she asked.

'Very sudden. Joe Rollins, my consultant, was go-ing to go, but his daughter's had rather a bad accident and I'm taking his place. It's all been very sudden. There are some new developments, new techniques in *in vitro* fertilisation. We need to know about them.'

'I see,' she said.

'Believe me, Emily, I don't want to go right now. There are things I have to…think about here.'

She believed him. And she felt just a little better.

Looking down, she discovered she'd drunk all her wine. When he tried to fill her glass she put her hand over it. Something told her that this was not a good time to be anything other than sober.

He seemed to change the subject. 'We've not really talked since you saw my father,' he said. 'It was good of you to say I could see his report.'

She tried to be light-hearted. 'My favour to you. You were entitled to know the results.'

But this was something he wanted to be serious about. 'And you're going to have the plastic surgery? You've got an appointment?'

She nodded. 'It came through today. It'll be a while before it's done—but I'm glad I decided.'

'Good. Should have had it done years ago.'

She realised suddenly that he was ill at ease. And that knowledge made her ill at ease, too. 'Perhaps you're right,' she muttered.

The question, when it came, was abrupt, even harsh. 'What about us, Emily? Have we a future?'

She didn't pretend she didn't know what he was talking about. She bowed her head. 'I don't know,' she said falteringly. 'I...like you a lot, Stephen.'

He went on, 'I'm sitting here, keeping my distance from you, when all I want to do is to be by you on that couch. I want my arms round you and I want...well, you know.'

He drank his wine. 'But just for once we'll both be detached. We'll talk and think, instead of being ruled by our feelings. Because feelings tend to go wrong, don't they, Emily? I know—or I think I know—what you feel for me. But we go so far and then you feel trapped. I know it, I can tell by the hunted look you get. I want you to give yourself to me fully, Emily. Just as I want to give myself to you. But can you do it?'

Now she did need a drink. She reached for her glass. He read her mind and leaned over to fill it.

How could she make sense of her turbulent thoughts? She tried to do as he'd suggested—be detached, think, instead of being ruled by her feelings. It should be possible.

She appreciated what he was doing. He was trying not to overwhelm her by the force of his feelings. She recognised that a man who was capable of doing that was very special. He deserved an honest answer. So, she realised, did she.

'You know my story. Well, for nearly three years now I've lived a frozen life. I've got on with my job and enjoyed it, but haven't allowed myself to feel much else. I think I've done some good. Every now and again, when delivering a baby, I've had a pang. I had a baby once, but that's in the past. Since then all that has mattered has been the job.

'I just haven't been interested in men. They could be colleagues, people I worked with, but they just didn't interest me. I was half frightened, half uninterested. Then I met you. I don't know why, but things seemed as if they could be different. I saw some kind of hope. But I was—I am—still frightened. I can't go through that agony of loving again. I'm scared of being hurt, even when I don't think I will be. Does that make sense?'

'Yes,' he said sadly, 'it makes sense.'

'You're right. I don't want anything to do with you unless it's a complete relationship. And I know I do care for you. I'll even say it—I think I love you.' She smiled shakily. 'In fact, I don't know which is more hurtful, having you or not having you.'

'I know which is hurting me more,' he said.

She wasn't sure what to say next. The decision was taken from her when his telephone rang. It was the call from America. She heard him discuss the course with the organiser, offer to take a couple of clinics, say how he was looking forward to trying the new technique.

In the tiny break she sipped her wine and tried to decide what to say. And finally she came to her decision. When he'd finished his call he looked at her silently. It was up to her.

'You're going away for three months,' she said. 'I shall miss you. While you're away I'll try to get rid of my demons. I can do it, Stephen. And, you know, there's nothing I want more than you. Silly, isn't it?'

'It's not silly. And I know you can come out on top.'

'And now I think I'd better go. You have to pack and you're off early.'

He came with her to the door, and she knew that if he asked her to stay she would. But he didn't—and she supposed she was glad. But he kissed her, a long kiss that started sweetly and finished, showing all the passion she knew burned inside him. His body was hard, muscular. She knew he was aroused but there was nothing she could do.

Finally it was he who reluctantly but urgently pushed her away. 'You have to go,' he gasped. 'You have to go now before it's too late. And, Emily, I didn't say it before but I love you.'

She stared at him, trying to get one fixed memory that would last her for three months of anguished waiting. It wasn't hard. She knew she couldn't forget him.

Then she went home. She didn't know whether she was elated or depressed. She only knew that things were different.

CHAPTER NINE

THREE days later Emily's life changed yet again. She was sent for by Dr Rollins, the ward's consultant gynaecologist and obstetrician. He was seen only seldom on the ward. Emily had seen far more of his specialist registrar—Stephen. Tapping at the door of his room, she felt a little apprehensive. A summons like this was bound to be about something important.

Dr Rollins was tall, lean, white-haired and aged about sixty. And he was kindness and courtesy itself. He sat her in a comfortable chair, poured her coffee and sat opposite her. 'I just wanted a chat, Emily,' he explained. 'I wanted to see how you were getting on since you joined us.'

Emily looked at him slightly askance. 'Consultants don't usually invite midwifes for coffee and a chat,' she said. 'In fact, some of them don't even know our names. There must be something else.'

The consultant looked a little taken aback. Then he recovered. 'Ah,' he said. 'Do you know, if there was a test here I'd say you'd just passed it.'

She looked confused. 'I'm not sure I follow you,' she said.

'Quite so.' He looked embarrassed. 'I telephoned Dr James yesterday for some advice about filling rather a difficult post. He recommended you. Without hesitation. I think I can now see why. You can obviously stand up for yourself.'

She was missing Stephen. It was exciting to hear someone else talking about him. And she got a thrill to think that he'd recommended her. She knew that no matter how much he loved her he wouldn't recommend her unless he meant it. Now she was truly curious.

'What kind of a difficult post?' she asked. 'You know I've only been working here for a few weeks.'

'I do know that.' Dr Rollins rose and indicated an area on a city map on his wall. 'You've not been here long, but do you know this area? It's called Hellington.'

'Commonly shortened to Hell,' Emily said, 'and with good cause. It's a vast sixties overspill estate. There used to be no end of work in the local factories but now they've all closed. Hellington is an offical "deprived area". We get a lot of mums from there.'

'You have a gift for summing up situations, Emily. You're quite correct.' He sat down again. 'Now, the hospital trust is opening a clinic there. As you say, there are lots of mums, and they're usually young, ill educated and seldom have a hus—that is, a live-in partner.' The consultant pronounced the phrase with some distaste and Emily tried not to smile.

He went on, 'The local GPs do a sterling job but we do need a clinic there. The mums can't easily get here, for a start. Anyway, we have a Dr Slater in charge of the natal section of the clinic and we need a senior midwife as well. We had appointed a very good person, a Miss Jeavons, to the post. I've known her for years. But we've just heard she's broken her leg, skiing.' The doctor sighed.

'Miss Jeavons will not be a happy lady. She was

looking forward to this work. But we can't have a midwife with her leg plastered up to the thigh.'

He looked at her sharply and she was suddenly aware that under the bumbling exterior there was a very keen mind. 'Will you be the midwife until Miss Jeavons can return? It'll be promotion, of course, but, I'm afraid, only temporary.'

Emily was a bit bewildered. Surely there were midwives with more experience than her? Why should she be singled out? She felt that there were things that weren't being said so she didn't accept at once. 'I'm really interested, but before I make a decision may I go to look around?' she asked.

'Of course,' Dr Rollins said gloomily.

She found out what hadn't been mentioned practically at once. Hellington Clinic—called simply that—was a new red-brick, single-storey building, surrounded by high-rise flats. There were flowers outside, but all the windows were protected by decorative but solid metal bars. Drugs were kept in clinics.

Inside there was a kind of amiable chaos. Furniture was piled up in the hall, people were wandering around, looking lost, and there was no notice on the front door. She found Dr Slater in his office, and immediately everything fell into place.

Dr Slater was a stooping man, aged about forty. He was running his hands through what remained of his hair, a gesture that Emily was going to learn to recognise. He looked harassed and, judging by the lines on his face, the harassed expression was almost permanent. With him was a young mum-to-be.

'If you could examine me now, Doctor, and sign

my form,' the new mum was saying, 'it would save
such a lot of time.'

Dr Slater looked dubiously at the proffered piece
of grubby paper. 'Well, we haven't really opened yet
Mrs—Miss Casey. I'm not sure that...I mean...'

'You could do it easily,' she pleaded. 'Can't you
make an exception just for me?'

'Well, perhaps just this once,' the doctor mumbled,
'but, really...'

'I'm Emily Grey, and I'm going to be the midwife
here,' Emily butted in. 'We're sorry, Miss Casey, but
we can't take any patients yet. Apart from anything
else, we're not insured. But I'll happily arrange an
appointment at Blazes for you.'

'Blazes is too far,' the girl whined. 'I can't get
there.'

'If you're in need, the hospital will arrange trans-
port. Now, how many weeks pregnant are you?'

'It doesn't matter. I'll come back when you're
open. If you ever are.' Angrily the girl slammed out
of the door.

Emily and Dr Slater looked at each other. 'Sorry,'
Emily said. 'Perhaps I shouldn't have interfered.'

The doctor shook his head. 'I'm so glad you did.
Occasionally the people around here can be so—
pressing. And one has to sympathise, though it sometimes leads to trouble.'

She knew what he meant. But she'd learned in
Africa that at times you had to be hard to be efficient.
Once rules were broken chaos followed inevitably.
The head must rule, not the heart.

'Are you really going to be the midwife?' the doctor asked eagerly. 'I had a very good understanding

with Miss Jeavons, but she's broken her leg, you know.'

'I know,' sighed Emily. 'And, if you'll have me, yes, I will be your new midwife.' Now she knew why the consultant had wanted her for the job, and why Stephen had recommended her. This place didn't need a midwife—it needed a manager. Dr Slater might be an excellent doctor but, in a phrase she'd heard her brother-in-law use, he couldn't organise a booze-up in a brewery.

Dr Slater smiled a trustful smile. 'When do you start? he asked.

'It's not up to me, but I'd like to start as quickly as possible. What arrangements have you made for the official opening?'

Dr Slater looked puzzled. 'Official opening?' he asked. 'D'you think we ought to have one?'

Three weeks later there was an official opening. There were representatives from the hospital, the community and the local press. Harry Shea and Ben Crosby were there so there was plenty of publicity. Emily knew that you had to be shameless about using your friends in this kind of work.

Dr Slater—he'd insisted she called him Jim—made a speech that was quiet but passionate. She realised that he was a caring man, a good doctor. He was just a poor manager. She decided they'd make a good team.

'We seem to have done quite well,' she said to Jim as they watched the caterers clear away the remnants of the buffet. 'You obviously impressed a lot of the local mums.'

He shook his head. 'You did quite well, Emily. I know my limitations. Organisation just isn't my big thing. The affair would have been a disaster without you.'

'Without us both,' she said.

It had been good to see Ben again. In the frantic rush to ready the clinic she'd had no time to go out with him, even though he'd phoned regularly. Now he, too, was starting work. They were shooting his part in the series, and he told her dolefully that he wouldn't be able to get out for quite a while.

'We'll still be friends, though?' he asked.

'Of course we will, Ben. But I think I—'

'You don't have to tell me,' he teased. 'It shows in your eyes, in the way you talk. Life's got suddenly better for you, Emily. You're in love.'

She blushed, but she didn't deny what he'd said. After all, it was true.

Work in the clinic was fun, but non-stop. She was out in the community much more, trying to carry the clinic's services to where they were needed most. She gave lectures on contraception at local schools, wincing when she thought what her old headmistress would have said. She tried to include some gentle suggestions about responsibility and love, but most of her talk was ruthlessly practical.

There were often woeful young mums-to-be to advise. At times she was appalled by their sheer ignorance. When she mentioned this on a trip to a local school the headmistress wasn't impressed. 'You ask us what we do,' she said flatly. 'The simple answer is that we do the very best we can.' It didn't take Emily long to find out she was telling the truth.

There were awkward officials to deal with. Sometimes she wondered if she was a midwife or a social worker. And there was the occasional belligerent father.

There was also the good side. Only when she helped Jim with his first clinic for neonates did she realise why he'd got this job. The man loved babies. He was a clever diagnostician, and surprisingly skilful in ferreting out relevant details from often uncommunicative mums. And when they got to know him, on their second or third visit, they all liked him.

'You're a push-over for babies,' she said accusingly, as they gratefully drank tea after their first exhausting clinic.

He smiled happily. 'I certainly am. I would have had half a dozen myself, but with me and Janet it just didn't happen.'

There were tragedies in all people's lives. Cautiously Emily asked, 'Did you...see if anything could be done?'

'Practically everything that medical science offers. Infertility clinics without number. But there comes a time when you have to realise that you're not going to be lucky. I accepted it, and I'm happy here. Janet's accepted it, too. She works with a playgroup and that gives her a lot of fulfilment.'

And I thought I had problems, Emily thought to herself.

Stephen phoned regularly. The first time it happened was completely unexpected. She was sitting at home, having her supper. 'Yes?' she asked indistinctly, her mouth half-full of egg sandwich.

His voice was warm, and so clear that he might have been in the next room. 'It's half-past three in the afternoon in Chicago, and the weather is scorching. I'm enjoying the course and my room is air-conditioned. I'm missing you, Emily.'

She was so shocked that at first she couldn't speak. 'Stephen!' she managed to splutter eventually when she'd swallowed her sandwich. 'I never thought you'd phone me.'

'Why shouldn't I phone you? Miracles of modern technology. It's good to hear your voice.'

'It's good to hear you, too, Stephen, but...you sound so close. And I know you're so far away.'

'Yes, I know.' His voice was wistful. 'I wish I was closer to you.'

'So do I. But I'm not. Tell me about the course.'

He did, and she was interested, but while he was talking she was sorting out something else in her mind. And it had to be said. Eventually he asked, 'What are you doing? How's the new job?'

'I'll tell you about how I'm enjoying the job,' she said slowly, 'but there's something difficult I've got to say first. Please don't angry.'

'I couldn't be angry with you, Emily.' Over that vast distance she could detect the wariness in his voice.

She tried to reassure him. 'I still..think a lot of you, and I think a lot about you, but I'm not very good at saying what I feel on telephones. It's hard enough to talk about feelings when I'm with you but I can't love a lump of electronic plastic, even if it has your voice.'

He laughed, and she felt relief pour through her.

She knew he understood. 'You're saying I'm not to worry if you sound a bit distant on the phone?'

'Something like that. It's good to hear from you, and I know we've got things to sort out, but I need to have you here to be able to talk to you properly. Could we just talk as friends for a while?'

'I understand. Now, tell me about the job. I knew you were the right person for it—just so long as you don't overdo things.'

'It's a challenge,' she said.

After that he phoned regularly. She looked forward to his calls. He talked of a world very different from the one she was inhabiting.

Rosalind came to the clinic to visit her—as ever, unexpected. She looked round, helped by holding a couple of babies and then insisted that Emily came out with her to a pub for lunch.

'I don't usually have a lunch break,' Emily explained as they sat, eating cheese salads, in the snug of the Dog and Gun.

'I know. It shows. You've lost a bit of weight again. You must keep eating. Are you enjoying the work?'

'I love it,' she said enthusiastically. 'My bossy side comes out a lot, I know, but I love it. And, really, compared with the organisation I had to do in Africa, this place is a doddle. Did I tell you about Granny Alert?'

Rosalind blinked. 'No,' she said.

'Well I've got a set of volunteer grandmothers who will come and help new young mums who haven't got anyone of their own. I vet them, of course, and I think they do something that we can't do. Even in the clinic the mums think we're the enemy. They spend so much time fighting officials that they think we're the same. But the grandmothers are like them, only a bit older.' In fact, the grandmothers tended to be about forty-five.

'Sounds a good idea. But it's extra work.'

'As I said, I like it.'

'I know where you get it from. Here's a letter from Dad. It arrived this morning.'

Delightedly Emily opened the creased pages, obviously torn out of some kind of exercise book. Like previous letters, it was addressed to all three of them. It was a comic letter, talking about his work and his problems. The guerillas had offered to release him but he had chosen to stay with them a little longer. He was doing some teaching. 'I was tired of just roaming,' he wrote. 'It's good to get in harness again, if only for a while, but I expect to be back with you before Christmas.'

'He's just like you,' Rosalind said, when Emily had read the letter twice. 'He's trying to find a life in work. But he knows he'll move on soon. There's more to life than work. Have you heard from Stephen?'

The apparent sudden change of subject confused Emily. 'What's that got to do with…? Yes, I have—why? How did you know that there's something between us?'

'I'm your sister, remember? Like Lisa? We know you and we love you. What about you and Stephen?' It was a typical Rosalind attack, concerned but ruthless.

'We…like each other a lot. When he gets back

we'll see what develops. I'm still a bit...wary of men.'

'It's obvious.' For a moment Rosalind devoted herself to her cheese salad, then she said abruptly, 'You know I never liked your husband? I never trusted him.'

Emily stared at her sister in alarm. Her dead husband was never mentioned. Why had Rosalind brought him up now? 'You never said,' she muttered.

'No point. You wouldn't have paid any attention, would you?'

'No,' she had to agree. 'Why are you dragging him up now?'

'I'm not. But I am telling you that I do like Stephen. So does Lisa. You'd be a fool to give him up because you made one stupid mistake.'

Emily winced. 'Aren't trainee doctors supposed to go on a course that teaches them how to approach patients with tact?'

'Been on it, passed it. You're too important for tact, sister mine. Stephen is the man for you. You've got to stop messing about and grab him.'

Emily wondered whether she should be angry or amused with her sister. Then she realised that neither was appropriate. Rosalind was right. 'I'm still frightened of committing myself,' she said. 'I don't know if I can.'

'You can, Emily. In fact, you've got to.' Rosalind smiled one of her rare smiles. 'I've got to get both my two sisters married off before I can look for a man myself. Now, time I was going.'

Having Rosalind for a sister was unsettling, Emily thought. But it made for an interesting life.

*   *   *

She had to make occasional home visits. There were some odd people hanging around here and there, but she found that if she moved confidently she wasn't bothered. The vast majority of people on the estate were decent and knew what she was doing. They would help if there was any trouble.

The Brents lived on the ninth floor of Cappen House, a great multi-storey block of flats. Doris Brent had two children already, Dale and Kevin. She was pregnant, with four weeks to go. She'd phoned in to cancel an appointment for no good reason, and Emily had decided to make a personal call. She wanted to keep an eye on Doris.

Doris was one of the women for whom the clinic was a godsend. It was so convenient. When she'd called in for an antenatal check-up Emily had seen desperation on her thin face. She could have done without this third child. 'It's Billy, my husband,' she confided as Emily wrapped the bandage round her arm to take her blood pressure. 'He's not got a job and he has trouble with his nerves.'

Emily knew this could well be true. Regular unemployment drove many men to mental illness. 'Has he been to see the doctor?' she asked.

'He won't go. He just sits around all day. And when he goes out—well, a man needs a bet.'

'You've got—money troubles?' she probed delicately.

But Mrs Brent had her pride. 'Everyone has money troubles round here,' she said.

The other thing about the estate was that everyone knew everyone else's business. Myra, their vast, pink-suited receptionist, seemed to act as the chief receiver

and dispenser of gossip. She was wise enough never
to mention anything medical, but anything else was
fair game.

Emily didn't like gossip, but often Myra could tell
her things that made a situation more understandable.

'Her old man's in deep with a moneylender,' she
whispered to Emily as Mrs Brent walked away. 'Lot
of the household money goes on paying him off. But
he's getting in deeper and deeper.'

Emily knew that there were unofficial money-
lenders on the estate, charging a ludicrous rate of interest. But there was nothing she could do. She wasn't
a social worker or the police.

She had to knock twice on the door of the Brents'
flat. A male voice growled inside. Finally, it was
Doris who opened the door, but cautiously kept on
the chain. 'It's you, Nurse,' she murmured. 'Come in,
then. I was lying down.'

Clutching her distended abdomen, Doris painfully
led the way back to her bedroom. Emily glanced
around quickly. There was little furniture in the room,
but there was a man—Billy Brent, she presumed—
sitting in the only easy chair.

Why hadn't he answered the door? Why had his
wife had to drag herself out of bed? 'Good afternoon,
Mr Brent,' she said in her most glacially correct voice.

Slowly he lifted his head to look at her, but didn't
speak at once. There was a long pause, then he muttered, 'Afternoon.'

Emily walked quickly into the bedroom. Doris was
her patient, not Billy. She was a midwife, not a mental
nurse. But she was sure that Billy was suffering from
more than simple 'nerves'. She remembered the few

162   A FAMILY AGAIN

weeks she'd once spent in a psychiatric ward when she was training to be a nurse. Her guess was that Billy was suffering from reactive depression.

Doris's pregnancy was progressing quite well. Emily checked her blood pressure, listened to the baby's heartbeat, did all the usual tests and checked that Doris was eating well. Physically there was nothing wrong. It was going to be a big baby, but both previous babies had been big, too. She arranged to call again in a fortnight, and ensured that Doris had a contact phone number for emergencies.

'Why did you cancel your appointment?' she asked. 'Not feeling too good?'

Doris shook her head and waved at the closed door. 'It's Billy. I don't like leaving him. And he won't come with me.'

Emily nodded. 'Has he been to see the doctor? He looks rather ill to me.'

Doris's face was bleak. 'He won't do anything. Just sits there and shouts at me if I try to talk to him. Then he seems to go mad and rushes out for an hour or so. I don't know what he does.'

'I really think he should see a doctor, Doris. Try to persuade him if you can.'

'You try. I've given up. I've got this baby to have.'

So Emily did try. She sat and talked to Billy for a while, noting the slowness of his responses—his unease at having to talk. After half an hour she felt she might have made some impression, but she wasn't a mental nurse. She decided to send a note to his GP and to the health visitor. It was really all she could do.

It happened two days later. She was just about to

start her morning clinic when Myra came in, her eyes flashing with excitement. 'The police are here and want to talk to you urgently. Say it's an emergency.'

It must have been an emergency because two policemen followed Myra, without being invited. She recognised the older one, Sergeant Travis. She'd spoken to him at the official opening and had found him friendly and helpful. But now his previously cheerful mouth was set in a hard, thin line.

'Miss Grey, we need to talk to you about Mr and Mrs Brent. I understand you spoke to them both two days ago?'

Emily ushered a fascinated Myra out of the room and shut the door firmly behind her. 'Yes, I did, but you must understand, Sergeant, that medical confidentiality—'

The younger policeman broke in impatiently. 'Medical confidentiality doesn't count now. We're trying to save the lives of his two kids. And perhaps his wife's as well.'

'What? Well, I...'

Irritated, the sergeant waved his colleague to silence. 'I'll explain and then perhaps you'll tell us if you can help in any way. We know Mr Brent has been having money problems. He's borrowed rather a lot from someone called Harry Appleton—he's a well-known local moneylender and drug-pusher. We've not been able to pin anything on him yet, but we know he's caused no end of misery.'

Sergeant Travis looked angry. 'If he'd come to us we might have helped but, instead, Billy Brent got a pistol from somewhere and when Harry called at the flat this morning Billy shot him. Harry's likely to die.

Billy's barricaded himself in his flat, and the kids and his wife are in there with him. He's still got the pistol. He says if we try to raid the place he'll kill all three.'

Emily had to sit down. 'How can I help?' she asked.

'What can you tell us about Billy? What was his mental state when you saw him? You're a nurse— you might have seen something that we can use. D'you think he'll shoot?'

There was a squawking sound from the radio on the younger officer's shoulder and he turned away to listen and mutter into it.

Slowly Emily said, 'Well, I'm not a qualified mental nurse but he did seem deeply depressed—'

'Sarge!' The younger officer interrupted. 'Just heard. Billy says his wife's having the baby. She's gone into labour but he still won't let anybody in.'

That decided Emily. 'You're going to need me,' she said. 'I'll get my bag and you can drive me there. Anything useful I can tell you I'll tell you on the way.'

The sergeant shook his head. 'This is police business now, miss, and it could be dangerous. If you'll hold yourself in readiness—'

'You're going to need a midwife at some stage. Now, let's stop wasting time and get there.'

It only took him a moment's thought. 'All right,' said the sergeant, 'but, remember, you do exactly as you're told.'

'I'm famous for that,' she muttered.

The clinic's policy was to try to encourage mothers to have their babies in hospital, but some still insisted on a birth at home and there had been more than a few emergencies when a mum had left things just a bit too late. Emily grabbed the bag that was kept ready for just this eventuality. She didn't need to check its contents. She knew what they were.

Jim wasn't in, which was a pity, but Emily knew that the ancillary staff could cope. She gave a gasped explanation to Myra and left, knowing that things would run smoothly for the rest of the day. She had organised this herself. Everyone had a typed sheet, telling them what to do in all foreseeable eventualities.

Then she was hustled into the police car and driven across the estate at an incredible speed. Sergeant Travis questioned her about Billy, but there wasn't much more she could tell him.

There was a small crowd outside Cappen House, and policemen guarded the entrance. Instinctively Emily glanced up at the ninth floor. There was a man in some kind of a blue uniform on one of the balconies near the Brents'. He seemed to be holding a gun.

'We've got two cordons round the flat,' the sergeant said. 'This is a hostage situation. We try to contain things and negotiate. The longer we can keep negotiations going the better our chances are. I'm just going to phone the superintendent in charge and ask if you can come up.'

'Tell him that I need to advise him about the mother,' Emily said.

There seemed to be policemen everywhere. The flats had been cleared above and below the ninth floor, and on the ninth floor itself the landing looked like a military command post. There were even three policemen with guns. Everyone wore a bullet-proof vest.

There were three telephones on a small table, and wires ran from them around the corner to the Brents' front door. A man with a gun was peering round the corner. Other policemen sat with earphones clamped to their heads.

'The midwife, sir,' said Sergeant Travis. 'Miss Grey—Superintendent Farrow.'

Emily found herself looking at a slight man who must have only just reached the minimum height for a policeman. Then she looked at the coldest blue eyes she'd ever seen behind silver-rimmed glasses. She could guess why this man had risen in the police force. He seemed to radiate authority.

'Miss Grey, good of you to come. I am in charge of this situation. I make all the decisions. While you are here you will do exactly as I tell you or you will be removed. Am I quite clear?'

'Quite clear,' Emily agreed. 'Do you deliver babies as well?'

The superintendent allowed himself the tiniest of smiles. 'As it happens, I have delivered three babies in my time in the force but I don't want to now. This is Sergeant Clements, who is our negotiator. What can you tell us about Brent that might be of help?'

There wasn't much she could tell them. She repeated what she'd said to Sergeant Travis and then asked, 'What can you tell me about Mrs Brent? How far has the labour gone?'

The superintendent frowned. 'We have a dedicated line here,' he said, indicating the wires going round the corner. 'We arranged to put it in as soon as we could. Clements has talked several times to Brent. He's managed to establish some kind of relationship.

Clements, do you think it would be an idea to tell Brent that the midwife is here? Suggest that his wife come out?'

'I'll try again, sir, but—'

'Ask him how frequent the contractions are,' Emily burst in. 'I need to know.'

Clements said nothing, but his eyes flicked to his chief. 'Yes, ask him,' he was told. 'Miss Grey, please remember I am in charge.'

She was surprised at the tone Clements used. It was friendly, easy, with none of the clipped efficiency he'd used when talking to his chief.

'Sorry to disturb you, Billy. Mike here. I just wanted to know how things are going... No, don't worry, we're not going to try anything stupid... Yes, we do believe what you say. The thing is, we've got the midwife here. She's asking about contractions... No, it's not a trick. We only want what's best for everybody.'

'Tell him I was here on Tuesday,' Emily whispered. 'My name's Emily Grey. Ask him if I can come in.' She didn't know why she said it. She only knew that someone needed to get into that room.

The superintendent frowned and pulled her away from Clements. He gestured to Clements, and Clements said, 'Well, I'll ring back in a minute. If you want a word, or if you want anything, you know I'm here. Everyone got plenty to eat? We can have some more stuff sent up.'

'Sir.' It was one of the men with the microphones who spoke. Somehow he'd heard Emily's question. 'I think the contractions are about every four minutes.

There's a regular pronounced difference in the breathing—I can hear her panting.'

'We've got microphones all round the flat,' the superintendent told her. We can hear everything that happens in there. We daren't just crash in. He's shot one person already, and he could still kill one or two of the children. In all hostage situations the longer we can put things off the better our chances of a happy outcome. And you can't go in. We're trying to release his hostages, not give him more.'

'You can't put off a birth,' Emily said. 'She might deliver the child herself successfully, but it's a risk I wouldn't take.'

For a second there was a flash of pain on that stone face. 'Don't think it's a choice I make easily, Miss Grey. I make any mistakes here—and I have to live with them afterwards.' He was human.

Behind them there was the sound of whispered argument, and then a voice she vaguely recognised said, 'Yes, I know there's a midwife there but I am a doctor and the woman is my patient. I may be able to help. If I may speak to the man in charge?'

There was too much happening. Emily wondered if she could cope. That voice…it couldn't be… But a figure came up the stairs and there was Stephen.

She had wondered about their next meeting and had looked forward to it, but she hadn't expected it to be on this brightly lit and ill-painted corridor, surrounded by policemen and with the threat of tragedy imminent.

He leaned forward and kissed her gently. With some part of her mind she recognised the lines of fatigue around his eyes. She guessed he'd flown in overnight.

'And who are you?' the superintendent asked brusquely.

Stephen didn't react to the harsh tone. 'I'm the hospital gynaecologist,' he said. 'I've examined this woman in the past. This midwife here is one of my staff. If there's a baby to be born, I'll be useful.'

'Nobody will be useful until we can get in that room,' the superintendent said. 'And that might not be for a while.'

'Ask if I can go in,' Emily urged again. 'I think he quite likes me. He might even trust me. He won't trust any of you.'

'No. We don't give him another hostage.'

'Then see if he'll swap me for the kids.'

'I think I'd be a better person to go in there,' Stephen put in. 'I have far more experience than Miss Grey.'

The superintendent looked at Stephen's obviously muscular body. 'He wouldn't let you in,' he said, 'not in a hundred years.'

'But he might let me in,' Emily pleaded. 'Why not ask?'

'Because he might shoot you,' the superintendent said brutally. 'He's high now. We have to wait for reaction to set in.'

Emily flinched. 'Mrs Brent will start probably screaming soon,' she said. 'What effect d'you think that noise will have on her husband?'

The superintendent considered. 'I hadn't thought of that,' he admitted. 'Clements?'

'Could push him over, sir. I can try and negotiate an exchange, if you wish, but I think it'll have to be the young lady.'

'Emily!' Stephen burst out. 'You can't...'

She reached and placed a hand gently over his mouth. 'Stephen, this is my decision. Please let me make it.'

She thought he was going to argue. His face became white. Then somehow he managed to smile. 'It's your decision,' he said. 'I won't interfere.'

'You're both wrong,' the superintendent said. 'It's my decision. And I—'

The officer with the headphones who had spoken before broke in again. 'The woman's screaming, sir.'

This time Emily remembered. 'May I listen?' she asked. When the superintendent nodded she took the headphones. The screaming had stopped. There was only the sound of sobbing and the faint complaint, 'Please, Billy, get somebody to help me. Please, Billy.'

'She's not delivering yet,' Emily said flatly, 'and she's asking for someone to help her.'

'See what you can do, Clements. Try to arrange an exchange.' The superintendent had made up his mind. Looking at his face, Emily couldn't guess what he was feeling.

'It's me again, Billy,' the friendly voice said. 'Look, is your wife not feeling so good? I've got a suggestion you might like to think about. Remember the midwife who called round a couple of days ago? I think you had a bit of a chat with her...'

Emily listened numbly to the conversation. She had volunteered to go into a room with a man who had just shot someone. He had threatened to kill his own children. At the moment he was volatile. Who could tell what he might do? Perhaps in a few minutes she'd be wheeled out of that room. Perhaps with a sheet pulled over her face.

She looked at Stephen. He looks like I feel, she thought. She knew what was passing through his mind. 'It'll be all right,' she croaked.

His smile was painful. 'Your decision, Emily.'

Clements had finished. 'You can go in, miss. He's letting one of the children out. Don't argue with him and do everything he says. He's close to the peak and he's liable to panic.'

'That makes two of us,' she muttered, but nobody laughed at her graveyard humour. She took one last look at Stephen's drawn face and walked alone down the corridor.

CHAPTER TEN

THE change-over had been carefully arranged. Only when the corridor was empty was Emily allowed to slide through the door. Then she had a gun forced against her ribs while Billy rummaged through her bag. Only then did he let one child go. Looking terrified, Dale ran through the door. Kevin, she was told, was asleep in the children's bedroom.

Billy piled the furniture back against the door. 'She's in there.' He gestured with the gun.

Emily entered the bedroom and the world she knew. 'Hello, Doris. It's Emily, the midwife—remember me? What's this, then? You're not due to have a baby for a while yet.' Her words sounded shrill and trite to Emily, but they appeared to give some comfort to her patient.

'What's Billy doing?' she asked. 'Are the children all right?'

'The children are fine,' Emily said reassuringly, 'and for the moment we'll forget about Billy. Let's have this baby, shall we?' She opened her black bag and took out a basic pack and sterile gloves. 'D'you want gas and air to ease the pain?' She reached for the Entonox.

It seemed as if it was going to be a straightforward birth. Once she had to hurry to the bathroom. Billy looked at her balefully but said nothing. The depression seemed to have left him, replaced by an energy that was far more frightening. And the gun was still in his hand. She ignored it and him, and carried on with her work. Assisting with the labour took her mind off the man with the gun.

Then things went wrong. The birth was imminent, the head clearly crowned. Now was the time to encourage Doris to push. But after twenty minutes there was no further progress. Emily decided to make a vaginal examination. Carefully, she felt past the baby's head. With a sick feeling she realised what the problem was. The baby's shoulders weren't rotating to the position for easy birth.

'Billy,' she called anxiously, and after a while he came to the door of the bedroom. She couldn't talk in front of her patient so for a moment Doris had to be left.

'Billy, we've got a problem,' she said desperately. 'The baby's in trouble. I can't manage. There's a proper doctor outside. I want him to come in.'

The gun flicked upwards and pointed straight at her. 'You're trying to trick me. You just want the police in here.'

'I'm not, Billy. We really do need—'

'Nobody else in here!' The voice rose to a shriek. She remembered what she'd been told about not exciting him.

'All right, Billy,' she said hastily, 'but do you mind if I talk to him on the phone? I need to ask what to do.'

For a moment the only sound was that of Doris's laboured breathing. Then he muttered, 'I'll bring the phone in here.'

'I need to talk to Dr James,' she said to Clements.

'I know. We can hear everything you say. You're doing well, miss. Dr James?'

She mustn't think of him as anything but a doctor. If she thought about the fact that this was the man she loved, the man she wanted to spend the rest of her days with, she wouldn't be able to cope with this nightmare. He was a doctor, that was all, and she was a midwife.

'Stephen, I have a problem,' she said calmly. 'I think we have a case of shoulder distocia. The baby isn't rotating.'

He knew what she needed. His voice was calm, formal. 'You have cut an episiotomy? You have the patient in the left lateral position?'

'Yes. I've tried the Willughby manoeuvre, I've tried to correct the position by rotating the shoulder forward and applying suprapubic pressure. I've not been successful.'

'I see. You haven't much time. Can you pass your hand round the back of the baby and rotate the shoulders through 180 degrees—so the posterior shoulder is anterior?'

This was not midwife's work, this was doctor's work. She tried—and was unsuccessful.

'I can't do it,' she said.

'Then we may have to try something else. That baby only has minutes left.'

She knew what he meant. The superintendent would give the order and the armed police would attack—with what result?

Although his voice was still calm, she felt she could detect the desperation underneath. 'One last thing,' he said. 'Try to deliver the posterior arm. Put your whole

hand into the sacrum. Get the baby's arm, flex the
elbow, pull the forearm over the chest and bring the
hand out. There should be no difficulty after you've
delivered the arms.'

It was something she'd never done. Again, it wasn't
a midwife's job. But she tried—and she did it. 'It's
working, going well,' she managed to gasp into the
phone.

After that things were straightforward. There was
only a depressed man with a gun in the next room.
She moved through the well-practised skills and then
there was a scream, half of joy, half of pain, from
Doris. The baby had been born.

She was fine. Emily wiped the mucus from the little
face and checked the respiratory effort. Then there
was the cord to clamp and cut.

Emily gathered the sticky armful. 'You've got a
lovely little girl,' she said. Quickly she wrapped her
in the towel she'd placed ready.

Then she took a decision that was to worry her for
years to come. She went to the door of the bedroom.
'Mr Brent,' she called.

He came over, the gun as ever in his hand. 'You
have a daughter,' Emily said, holding out the bundle.
'Now, d'you want to give me the gun?'

He looked at her for the longest minute of her life.
Then he stooped to place the gun on the floor and
reached for his child. 'Shall I open the front door?'
Emily asked, and he nodded. He walked into the bedroom, still holding the baby.

Emily picked up the phone. 'I'm unlocking the
door and putting the gun into the corridor,' she told

Clements. 'Don't let everybody rush in. I think the crisis is over.'

'Yes, miss, but we have come for him.'

'Ask Dr James to come in as well,' Emily said. Then, with her blood-stained gloves, she picked up the gun.

Two of the armed policemen came in first. One of them quickly went to the children's bedroom and carried out Kevin, still apparently half asleep. Then the two of them waited cautiously until Emily went into the bedroom. The baby was lying on her mother's breast, and Billy was looking down at his wife and new child.

'You'll have to go now,' Emily said. He nodded, and after one last look at the couple in bed he walked out. The policemen were firm but not unnecessarily brutal. Billy was searched and handcuffed, before being led out. Then Stephen hurried into the room.

'Everything seems to be fine,' she said shakily, 'but I'd like you to have a look.'

'Of course. There's an ambulance outside. We'll have her in hospital inside an hour. But we'll have a quick examination first. Has the placenta been delivered?'

Both of them knew it would be easiest if they kept up the pretence of this being a normal birth. She knew she couldn't manage for much longer, but she'd hold out until she could hand over her charges to trained and equipped paramedics.

She decided not to clean up mother and child. It would be done more easily in hospital. She put the little girl to her mother's breast, and gently rubbed the nipple against the damp cheek. She always loved watching a tiny mouth hunting for food for the first time.

'What about Billy?' Mrs Brent asked faintly.

'He's been taken away,' Stephen said softly. 'He won't hurt himself or anyone else.'

'It wasn't all his fault, you know. He got a bit bothered. He loves us, really.'

'He probably needs hospital treatment. We'll see he gets it,' Stephen promised. 'Now, everything seems fine down below. There's a stretcher here and an ambulance to drive you to hospital. Don't worry about the children, either. We'll see they are looked after.'

'Thank you, Doctor. And you Emily.'

There was a rattle outside, and a green-coated man and another midwife entered with the wheeled stretcher. Emily gave a swift report to the woman as Stephen and the man lifted Mrs Brent onto the stretcher. Then Mrs Brent was gone.

Emily looked at the shabby bedroom, the blood-soaked sheets. Slowly she took off her apron. There was a world and a life for her outside this. She glanced at her fob watch. It was half past twelve! She'd been here only two hours.

The superintendent came in. 'Don't think about going back to work, Miss Grey,' he said. 'Take my word for it, you just won't manage. I've arranged for a police car to take you both home. There's a lot to be said and there'll be an awful lot of paperwork, but it can wait till tomorrow. Miss Grey, you know we owe you our thanks. There's nothing a policeman hates more than guns.'

'He wasn't really a bad man,' she said.

The superintendent wasn't having this. 'He held a loaded gun against an innocent person. There are few things worse than that.' Then he appeared to think again. 'But we've just heard that Harry Appleton probably won't die so Billy won't face a murder charge. Now, you two go home. Social Services are standing by. We'll sort out this mess.'

'Thank you, Superintendent,' Stephen said.

He put his arm around Emily as they were guided to the lift, taken out of the front door and handed into a police car. 'Please put on your safety belts,' the driver said. 'Now, where can I take you?'

Stephen took charge. 'We'll go to my flat,' he said.

She knew what was happening. She was suffering from shock. Her skin was cold and clammy and she knew her pulse was low volume. She felt confused.

'What are you doing home, Stephen?' she asked irritably. 'I thought you were in America for another six weeks.'

'I am. But I've got four days off. I decided to fly here to see you.'

'Four days off? And you've flown from America?' America was so far away that the idea seemed insane.

'Why not? I've missed you. I arrived early this morning, dropped my bags at the flat and came straight out to see you. I wanted to surprise you. And then you surprised me.'

'I'm sorry,' she said. 'I'm sorry.'

The policeman escorted them to the front door of Stephen's flat. By this time she felt so tired that she hardly knew what she was doing. Vaguely she recognised the living room and saw the open door to his bedroom. Inside, an open case lay on the bed. 'Sit here,' he said, and lowered her onto his couch. It was so soft that she seemed to sink into it for ever.

He fetched her tea, hot, strong and sweet. She pulled a face. 'Medicine,' he said, 'so drink it. We're getting your blood sugar up.' Then he sat next to her and put his arm round her.

It was so comfortable there, so warm, that she wanted to sleep. But Stephen wouldn't let her. 'Drink your tea,' he urged, 'like I am.'

'Bet it's not as horrible as mine.'

'Bet it is. Here, try.' She sipped from the cup. It *was* just as horrible as hers. 'I'm in shock, too,' he said. 'Emily, d'you know what it was like, watching you go in that door? To face what I thought was a murderer with a gun?'

'I think I had it easier,' she said, and then she burst into tears.

He held her as the sobs shook her body, and the terror she'd managed to control finally found its outlet. Eventually the fit passed and she lay back and sighed. She felt weak but she felt better. 'I must look a mess,' she said. She looked down at her stained uniform and winced. 'I should have changed.'

'I'll make you another cup of tea. Why don't you go and have a bath? Then I'll cook something for you.'

'Cook something for me?' Suddenly it struck her. She was hungry. 'I'd like that,' she said.

'While you're in the bath I'll do a bit of phoning around. There are things I want to know, people I need to tell about you. The other two Grey sisters for a start. I don't want them hearing anything on the news.'

'No,' she said, and let him lead her to the bathroom.

His bath was bigger than hers and, after filling it, he sprinkled the water with liberal amounts of some aromatic bath oil. It was a very masculine smell but she liked it. As she lay there luxuriously, only her face and the tips of her knees showing above the water, he tapped on the door and entered to scoop up her clothes. How strange. She must have forgotten to lock the door. 'There's a dressing-gown for you,' he said. 'A bit big but it will do.'

She lay there for another half-hour. She could feel the tension draining from her. Now she could look back on the events of the morning and judge them more dispassionately. And one fact, one question, loomed larger and larger—became more and more significant. Stephen had come home—just for four days, he'd said. Why?

Finally, reluctantly, she climbed out of the bath, patted herself dry with the warm towels provided and pulled on the dressing-gown. Where were her clothes?

Stephen was sitting on the couch, and stood as she entered. She walked across to him. 'I bet that's the suit you flew across the Atlantic in,' she said. 'It's crumpled.' She put her hands to his face, stroked his cheeks. 'You haven't shaved either. But you got here and you came straight out to see me. Why?'

'I'll tell you later,' he said. 'There's a tray for you in the bedroom. Why don't you get into bed and eat what I've made for you? Rosalind is going to come round this evening and bring you some clothes. But right now it's my turn for a bath.'

'I don't mind you all scruffy,' she said. 'I really don't.'

'You haven't spent hours in a plane. I'll see you in half an hour.' He disappeared into the bathroom.

The case had been removed and the bed turned down. It seemed the most natural thing in the world to slide between the sheets and pull the tray onto her lap. He'd obviously had no fresh food, but with the next cup of tea he'd heated her a tin of salmon and asparagus soup and there was toasted cheese on rye-bread crisps.

She ate. She knew now why she felt so tired, even though it was only early afternoon. It wasn't an uncommon occurrence after great emotional trauma to feel physically exhausted. She had seen fathers who would sit up indefinitely with their wives in labour but as soon as the baby was born, and they knew that mother and child were doing well, they'd collapse and sleep anywhere.

She finished the soup and crisps, and put the tray at the side of the bed. Stephen was still in the bath so just for a minute, she'd close her eyes. Sighing with the sheer bliss of it, she pulled the duvet to her chin and slid down the bed.

This wasn't her bed. Puzzled, Emily opened her eyes. That wasn't her ceiling either. Slowly recollection came flooding back—the siege in the flat, Stephen's return, the bath in his flat. She'd gone to sleep in his bed. Judging by the shadows on the ceiling, she'd slept for quite some time.

She rolled over to look at the clock on his bedside table, and blinked. There was a man in bed with her. To be exact, she was in the bed and Stephen was lying on the top. He had on a tracksuit and leather slippers.

For a moment she lay there and listened to his steady breathing, looking at his face. She'd never seen him asleep before. He was relaxed. His face appeared less stern, more vulnerable than usual. He must have been more tired than me, she thought. She remembered that it was always more tiring to wait anxiously than actually to do something.

Her sleep had refreshed her. She felt wide awake, full of energy. The darkness of the morning's happenings had disappeared. Carefully she wriggled upwards, then leaned over and kissed Stephen softly on the lips. There was an odd delight in being the aggressor, being able to take the initiative.

His breath was warm and sweet, and she kissed him again. From somewhere an arm slid round her waist and pulled her closer. 'You're supposed to be asleep,' she said accusingly.

'I'll go back to sleep if you'll kiss me again.' He didn't let her go so she kissed him again.

'Aren't you cold,' she asked after a while, 'perched there on the top of the bed?'

'I'm all right. I didn't want you to wake up and be alarmed. In fact, I didn't intend to sleep at all. It just crept up on me.'

'Me, too.' The decision was taken quickly, without any conscious thought. She pushed down the duvet. 'Here, climb inside. It's warmer.'

'But—'

'No buts. Just do it.' So he did.

For a while they just lay there, looking at each other. Then she made another decision, again without any thought of possible consequences. She was wearing his dressing-gown, a long maroon towelling one,

which was far too big for her. She undid the belt and
wriggled her arms out of the sleeves. He reached over,
slipped the gown from her shoulders and pushed it
back. She lay there, naked.

He placed the tip of his finger on her forehead and
traced a slow line downwards—along her nose, her
half-opened lips, her chin and throat and then the soft
valley between her breasts.

'You're still dressed,' she said plaintively. 'Take
off your tracksuit.'

His hands reached for her and pulled her to him.
One hand cupped her neck, the other stroked her back.
His kiss was fierce, passionate, his tongue probing
deep in her mouth, as if he wanted their bodies so
close together as to be practically one. She recognised
his need for her, and responded with her own need.
'I thought I might lose you,' he groaned eventually.
'Nothing I've ever done hurt like waiting outside that
door.'

'I know,' she muttered, 'I know. But we're safe
now. And...' Her hand tugged at his tracksuit.

Infinitely slowly he pushed her away. 'Emily, are
you sure you want...? That is, you might be...'

Deftly she unzipped his jacket. 'You think I'm still
in shock from this morning and that I don't know
what I'm doing. That's not so. I do know what I'm
doing, I know what I want. I want you. Now take off
these clothes!'

He did. They were naked in bed together. For one
moment she wondered if she could do this, or if some
hidden fear would surface to crush her with its cold
hand again. It didn't. At long last she was free of her
inhibitions and the nightmare of her past.

He leaned over to kiss her again but this time more gently, as if he had all the time in the world. The fine hair on his leg rubbed against hers, the muscles of his chest pressed against her breasts and she felt their burgeoning tips. She moaned as his lips caressed hers, and then moved lower down her body. Her back arched. 'Do that again,' she moaned.

It was all so easy. Her body was in tune with his mounting desire. Instinctively she knew what he wanted—it was what she wanted, too. When he was above her she opened herself to him, sighed at the sweet penetration then joined with him in a frenzied climax.

'Thank you,' she whispered when the storm of passion was over, then slept in his arms.

This time it was the smell of coffee that woke her. Somehow, without her knowing, he'd slid out of bed, taken his cast-aside dressing-gown and gone to the kitchen.

He slid beside her again, and handed her a mug. 'Rosalind will be here in an hour,' he said. 'I think we have to talk. '

'Don't want to talk. I want to do things.'

He kissed her. 'We will do things, but later. Emily, you had problems. They've gone now?'

'They've gone,' she confirmed. 'If I can risk having a man push a gun at me then I can risk a relationship.'

'So it was this morning that decided you?'

She shook her head. 'Not really. I'd already decided that I loved you, and that I'd try like mad to make sure everything went well. This morning made me realise what I might be missing. I made one mistake, forming a relationship with somebody unsuitable. It would be an equally big mistake not to form a relationship with someone who was very suitable.'

'Relationship?' he queried.

She blushed. 'It's for you to decide what it should be. We've only really just got to know each other.'

'I don't agree. I think I've known you for ever.'

'We will know each other for ever,' she sighed. 'I promise you, we will.'

Your Special Christmas Gift

Three romance novels from Mills & Boon® to
unwind with at your leisure—
and a luxurious Le Jardin bath gelée to pamper
you and gently wash your cares away.

for just £5.99

Featuring
Carole Mortimer—Married by Christmas
Betty Neels—A Winter Love Story
Jo Leigh—One Wicked Night

MILLS & BOON®

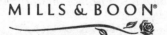

Makes your Christmas time special

Available from 23rd October 1998

CHRISTMAS

Affairs

MORE THAN JUST KISSES UNDER THE MISTLETOE...

Enjoy three sparkling seasonal romances by your
favourite authors from

MILLS & BOON®
Presents™

HELEN BIANCHIN
For Anique, the season of goodwill has become...
The Seduction Season

SANDRA MARTON
Can Santa weave a spot of Christmas magic for Nick
and Holly in... *A Miracle on Christmas Eve?*

SHARON KENDRICK
Will Aleck and Clemmie have a... *Yuletide Reunion?*

MILLS & BOON®

Makes any time special™

Available from 6th November 1998

MARGOT DALTON

second thoughts

To Detective Jackie Kaminsky it seemed like a routine
burglary, until she took a second look at the
evidence... The intruder knew his way around
Maribel Lewis's home—yet took nothing.
He *seems* to know Maribel's deepest secret—
and wants payment in blood.

A spellbinding new Kaminsky mystery.

1-55166-421-6
**AVAILABLE IN PAPERBACK
FROM OCTOBER, 1998**

Jennifer
BLAKE

KANE

Down in Louisiana, family comes first.
That's the rule the Benedicts live by.
So when a beautiful redhead starts paying a little
too much attention to Kane Benedict's grandfather,
Kane decides to find out what her *real* motives are.

*"Blake's style is as steamy as a still July night...as overwhelming
hot as Cajun spice."*

—Chicago Times

1-55166-429-1
**AVAILABLE IN PAPERBACK
FROM OCTOBER, 1998**

FIND THE FRUIT!

How would you like to win a year's supply of Mills & Boon® Books—FREE! Well, if you know your fruit, then you're already one step ahead when it comes to completing this competition, because all the answers are fruit! Simply decipher the code to find the names of ten fruit, complete the coupon overleaf and send it to us by 30th April 1999. The first five correct entries will each win a year's subscription to the Mills & Boon series of their choice. What could be easier?

A	B	C	D	E	F	G	H	I
15					20			

J	K	L	M	N	O	P	Q	R
	25						5	

S	T	U	V	W	X	Y	Z
		10					

4	19	15	17	22

15	10	3	17	15	18	3

2	19	17	8	15	6	23	2	19

4	19	15	6

4	26	9	1

7	8	6	15	11	16	19	6	6	13

3	6	15	2	21	19

15	4	4	26	19

1	15	2	21	3

16	15	2	15	2	15

C8J

Please turn over for details of how to enter ➜

HOW TO ENTER

There are ten coded words listed overleaf, which when decoded
each spell the name of a fruit. There is also a grid which contains each
letter of the alphabet and a number has been provided under some
of the letters. All you have to do, is complete the grid, by working out
which number corresponds with each letter of the alphabet. When
you have done this, you will be able to decipher the coded words to
discover the names of the ten fruit! As you decipher each code, write
the name of the fruit in the space provided, then fill in the coupon
below, pop this page into an envelope and post it today. Don't forget
you could win a year's supply of Mills & Boon® Books—you don't
even need to pay for a stamp!

Mills & Boon Find the Fruit Competition
FREEPOST CN81, Croydon, Surrey, CR9 3WZ
EIRE readers: (please affix stamp) PO Box 4546, Dublin 24.

Please tick the series you would like to receive if you
are one of the lucky winners
Presents™ ❏   Enchanted™ ❏ Medical Romance™ ❏
Historical Romance™ ❏ Temptation® ❏

Are you a Reader Service™ subscriber?   Yes ❏   No ❏

Ms/Mrs/Miss/Mr ....Initials ....
(BLOCK CAPITALS PLEASE)

Surname...

Address ....

....

....Postcode.........................

(I am over 18 years of age)   C8J